Whispers of Starlight

Book Three in the Whispers of New England Series

SUE MILLS

Choose The Front Row Media

Published by Choose The Front Row Media

Contact: choosethefrontrow@gmail.com

Cover Design by Emily Hensley of smallfrymarketing.com

Editing and Proofreading by Red Adept Editing Services

Paperback ISBN: 979-8-9918300-7-2

"This read feels akin to cozying up in a blanket by the fireplace on a cold winter day—its passionate romance tugs at the heartstrings yet maintains suspense with certain twists that readers may not expect."

Author's Note

THANK YOU FOR PICKING up *Whispers of Starlight.*

This is the third book in the Whispers of New England series. *Starlight* and *Whispers of Mistletoe,* the second book in the series, form a duet, and although both books are independent, knowing Mistletoe's story will enhance your enjoyment.

To give some background, Quinn Michaels is a twenty-nine-year-old nurse working in Hanover, New Hampshire. In *Whisper of Forgiveness,* the first book in the series, she is attending a conference in Boston and Sam Carpenter, the high school boyfriend who broke her heart ten years earlier, sits next to her on the first day. While they are becoming reacquainted, she also meets Caden Brady, a charismatic doctor who lives in Boston.

Whispers of Mistletoe is the story of Caden and Quinn's courtship during the period between Thanksgiving and Christmas. They fall in love, but trauma in Caden's past, and the continued presence of Sam in Quinn's life complicate that love.

Whispers of Starlight, opens on New Year's Eve, and explores how a relationship grows more complex when life intrudes, and that first blush of love fades before growing into a deeper connection.

Playlist

Auld Lang Syne – The New Year's Anthem – Mariah Carey

All My Love – Coldplay

Euphoria – BTS

The Astronaut – Jin

I Love You 3000 II – 88rising, Stephanie Poetri, Jackson Wong

Eyes Off You – PRETTYMUCH

golden hour – JYKE

universe – thuy

double take – Dhruv

Meet Me in Amsterdam – RINI

3:00 AM – Finding Hope

I Like Me Better – Lauv

Die With A Smile – Lady Gaga, Bruno Mars

You Are in Love (Taylor's Version) – Taylor Swift

Contents

Chapter One
New Year's Eve

Quinn

QUINN PARKED IN FRONT of the address Caden had given her and sent him a text. Coming out quickly, he took her bag inside, came back, and motioned her to move to the passenger seat. He slid behind the steering wheel and leaned over to give her a kiss before driving to the parking garage.

Caden hopped out of the car and hurried to the passenger side to open the door. Quinn stayed seated, having learned to enjoy this pampering from him. He took her hand as she climbed out, then pulled her close. "I've missed you," he whispered, just before bringing his lips to hers. His hands moved up and down her back before he let her go with a sigh. "It's a fifteen-minute walk. Is that okay?"

"Absolutely." At the hospital, she had changed into jeans, a heavy sweater, and sneakers. He slid his arm around her waist as they walked, and she was happy to fall in beside him. "This is nice. The only time we've walked like this was that hike way back on our first weekend together." Quinn snuggled closer to him.

"We'll do plenty of walking while you're here. I seldom use my car."

"I'm glad the decorations and lights are still up. It's so pretty. You can't believe how excited I am to see the inside of one of these brownstones. And I'm going to stay there? Oh man, that's over the top."

"So it's not me. It's my brownstone you're excited about," Caden teased.

"You're the cherry on the sundae," she assured him. "That first night you texted me and told me where you lived? I couldn't believe I'd met someone who lives here. I took an intro to architecture class in college, and I geek out over buildings."

They arrived at his address and paused before they walked in to give Quinn a chance to study the building. When Caden opened the door, she drew in a sharp breath. They were facing large French doors that led to a terrace with the city lights twinkling in the distance. "Can we go out there?" Quinn breathed.

Caden opened the door and held her hand as they stepped out. There was an iron chaise with a dark gray cushion and an iron bistro table. The cushions on the two chairs matched the gray on the chaise.

Quinn walked to the outer wall, which was brick, and came to her chest. "Does this wall make you feel secure?" He nodded with a grin. "Do you spend much time out here? I'd eat every meal out here in the summer."

"I do." Caden joined her at the wall. "It's a nice place to relax." He put his arm over her shoulder, and they gazed out at the city they both loved. "We should get ready."

Back inside, Quinn shook her head in wonder as she looked around the living room. The walls were sage with light colored hardwood floors which gleamed. The elaborately carved wood-work was dark, and his furniture was chocolate brown.

"This is spectacular. Did you decorate it yourself? It's so you."

"My friend Danny's wife is a decorator. She helped me. I'm glad you like it." He took her coat off, then moved his hands under her sweater.

Quinn melted into him, sighing. "We don't have time for this, do we?"

He shook his head and pulled back. "No, we don't. Let me show you the bedrooms. I thought you might want your clothes in the guest room. It'll give you some privacy to get ready."

"Do you have many guests?"

"I'm hoping I'll have one on a regular basis." Caden winked at her. "But she'll be in my bedroom." He led her to the upper level, where there were three bedrooms and a den.

She did her hair and makeup the same as she had for the Christmas dinner with her friends a few weeks earlier, slipped on her dress and shoes, and returned to the living room where he was waiting, dressed in a black suit with a red tie. She smiled, delighted. "Wow, you look even more handsome than usual!"

"And you look as gorgeous as you did that night in the guesthouse." His blue eyes were warm on hers. "I don't even dare kiss you because I know I'll mess up your makeup. But I'll be thinking all night about what we'll be doing when we get home."

"Mmm, so will I."

They took a rideshare to the hotel, and once inside, Quinn started following the sign to the ballroom, only for Caden to hang back.

"Quinn, wait up."

She turned to find him a few steps behind her, an odd expression on his face. She walked back, and he took her hand in his.

"Inevitably, someone tonight, after several drinks, is going to tell you how great it is to see me happy," he said, voice low. "My money's on one of the women, but hell, it might even be one of the guys. They've seen me at my worst. If they try to talk to you about it, can you tell them I haven't shared all the details, and you'd rather not talk about it until I do?" He ran his hand through his hair. "Christ! I don't know. I'm putting you in an awkward position."

This was a different side of Caden, not the self-assured, handsome doctor Quinn had fallen in love with. He looked more vulnerable than she had ever seen, including even the night she'd told him about Sam.

Quinn raised her hand to his cheek. "Caden, it'll be fine. Thanks for warning me. I don't want details about your life from anyone but you. I'll handle it. Let's go have fun."

They walked into the dimly lit ballroom, where tall trees draped with white lights sparkled all around the dance floor. The tables for six boasted white tablecloths with red overlays and three pillar candles blazing. A string quartet played softly in one corner. When someone motioned them over, Caden waved and started walking in his direction.

At the table, he introduced Quinn and reeled off his friends' names, starting with Danny and Brooke.

Quinn raised her hand in greeting. "Forgive me if I mix up your names."

Danny spoke up. "Just concentrate on Brooke and me. I'm his oldest friend."

Across the table, the guy she knew must be Robbie shook his head. He had shaggy blond hair and stood as he said, "How's the evening going to go if you are this obnoxious already? All you need to remember, Quinn, is Danny is the short redhead, and I have even Cade beat in the height department." He reached out for Quinn's hand, saying as he shook it, "It's nice to meet you, darlin'."

Danny groaned. "Oh God, starting with the southern charm already."

The two women at the table rolled their eyes at each other. Robbie's wife, Jennifer, had long blond hair piled on top of her head and wore a green dress. Brooke's dress was silver, and she wore her brown hair down. Both women stood to greet them, and Brooke gave Caden a kiss on the cheek.

Caden led her to the bar. "You understand that's good-natured ribbing between them?"

Quinn nodded.

"I didn't think you'd like me leaving you there alone. You want white wine?"

"You are correct, and I need something stronger than wine. Get me a margarita."

"Seriously? I've never seen you drink tequila."

She raised one trembling hand to show him. "Oh, I'm serious. I'm very intimidated, and I need something to relax me."

He put his arm around her. "You're not that quirky teenager from northern Vermont. You're an accomplished nurse, a woman who has lived all over the country by herself. Most of my friends are like me. They've never lived over ten miles from Boston. Plus, you look stunning. You have nothing to be intimidated about."

She sighed, but realized she felt a little better. "How do you do that? Get right to the heart of my insecurities?" A corner of her mouth lifted. "I still want tequila."

They returned to the table, and Quinn sat between Caden and Brooke with Robbie and Jennifer on Caden's other side. Brooke drew Quinn out, asking her about working at Dartmouth and letting her know she was the one who decorated Caden's brownstone.

"It's so gorgeous." Quinn said. "It really reflects him."

"Cade was probably the easiest client I've ever had. He knew what he wanted, but he always listened to my suggestions, too." Brook snickered. "And of course, the unlimited budget didn't hurt either."

Unlimited budget! Wow, as opposed to me, who plans one project a year. "Has he told you about the guesthouse he stays in when he comes to Hanover?" When Brooke shook her head, Quinn continued. "It's beautiful, like an overgrown dollhouse, and it has a fantastic bathroom."

"Have you met any of his family?"

"Just Claire and James. And of course, Rory." Quinn hesitated. "We're going to his parents' for dinner on Saturday. I'll confess I'm a little nervous."

"Don't be," Brooke reassured her. "They're great. Very close knit. You'll like them."

Between Brooke's friendliness and the tequila, Quinn's tension eased. After dinner, the quartet gave way to a band, and the music ranged from sixties to contemporary. Caden led her to the dance floor, where she admired his moves. When a slow song started, she melted into his arms and said, "I'm having so much fun." Liquor flowed freely, which Quinn was sure contributed to the carefree atmosphere. Wine was served with dinner, everyone had more cocktails while the band was playing, and champagne would be served at midnight.

Caden

When the band returned from a break, Danny took Quinn's hand. As he led her to the center of the ballroom, he said, "Cade, you owe Brooke a dance, and I want to dance with your lady."

Caden took Brooke's hand, but his eyes were on Quinn. When she threw back her head in laughter at something Danny said, the same sensation he'd had when Quinn told him about Sam staying in her guest room overcame him. His heartbeat wildly, and his ears clanged. He started sweating and felt like he couldn't breathe. Pictures from the Natick house flashed even when he squeezed his eyes shut, trying to dispel them.

"Caden, what's wrong?" Brooke asked. "Let's get some fresh air." She led him to the terrace.

Once they were outside, he bent over and took several breaths. He turned away from Brooke. *Jesus, get a grip.* The pictures faded and his heart calmed. Slowly, he turned back to face Brooke, who was staring at him with a serious look on her face.

"What's going on? Do you have a problem with Danny dancing with Quinn? We've always danced with everyone."

"Rationally, I know that. I have some kind of crazy reaction to the idea of Quinn with another man." He continued taking deep breaths.

"Cade, it's not another man. It's Danny."

"I know that. It's irrational and comes out of the blue."

"Has it happened before?"

"Once." *Do I want to share what happened in December? She and Danny know everything about me.* "A few weeks ago, she let an ex-boyfriend sleep in her guest room."

Before he could explain, Brooke interrupted, "Her ex-boyfriend? Seriously?"

"Hold on. She explained." Brooke's support for him brought a smile to his face. He shared what Quinn had told him about that night Sam slept off a bender at her townhouse. "She told me about it the next day, with no prompting. I didn't even ask a question. I trust her Brooke." He ran his hands through his hair. "But I reacted like what you just saw." The doubt on her face was easy to read. "She's told me everything about that relationship. I have nothing to worry about. So don't be all mama bear on me."

"I couldn't stand to see you hurt again."

"I know." He nodded. "I'm okay now. Can this stay between us, please?"

Brooke made a zipping motion in front of her lips. "I thought she seemed great, very genuine...but now..."

"Your first instinct was correct. She's amazing."

"Have you told her what happened with Mary?"

"Not yet. Planning to do it tomorrow."

They spent a few minutes more on the terrace, and when they walked inside, Quinn and Danny were back at the table, talking to Robbie and Jennifer. Caden took Quinn's hand, leading her to the dance floor as a slow song started. He held her tightly, and at the end of the song, they went to the terrace. She melted against him, and they shared a long kiss.

Caden said softly, "I've been wanting to do that all night."

The band led a countdown to midnight, when Caden kissed and hugged Quinn again. He whispered in her ear. "This is going to be an exceptional year."

Quinn took off her shoes as soon as they were inside the brownstone and climbed the stairs barefoot. This struck both of them as funny, and they giggled all the way up. As soon as the door closed behind them, Caden threw his arms around her and she jumped onto him, wrapping her legs around his waist. He carried her to his bedroom and laid her on the bed. Pushing her dress out of the way, he removed her thong and lowered his face between her legs. His tongue darted into her folds and found her clit. First one, then two of his fingers slid inside as he licked her.

"Oh, Cade, what are you doing to me?" She thrust against his face while his tongue continued to play with her clit and his fingers plunged in and out. Her low moan started, and his pressure increased until her climax exploded. He gently stroked her until the waves stopped.

In the aftermath, Caden unbuttoned his shirt and tossed it on a chair. He enjoyed Quinn's gaze on him as he unbuckled his belt and shoved his pants to the floor. She held out her arms, beckoning to him with the deep brown eyes that he loved. Gently lifting her off the bed, he unzipped her dress and eased it off. Lying next to her, he circled her nipple with his tongue while she stroked his cock. The heat between them rose quickly, and he rolled on a condom from a box next to the bed. She climbed on top of him, taking him deeply, then rising almost all the way off. Her teasing drove him wild.

Caden reached toward her hair, removing the pins, and loving how the waves cascaded down past her shoulders. He pushed up on his elbows so he could reach her nipple again, knowing that would send shock waves throughout her body and put a halt to the torture. His climax was rising, and he screamed her name as it hit. Her orgasm followed, and she collapsed on top of him. He wrapped his arms around her, not wanting to break their connection.

Caden dragged the covers over them, but after a few minutes, Quinn rolled off the bed and stumbled to the bathroom. He heard her retch, and followed her, then held her hair back as she kneeled in front of the toilet, vomiting up all the alcohol from the evening. *I don't think she even knows I'm here.*

When her stomach was empty, she leaned back and bumped against him. "Oh God, that was romantic, huh? I don't assimilate alcohol very well. I know better than to drink so much."

He gave her a washcloth to wipe her face. "Not a problem. You okay now? Is there more to come?"

"God, I hope not. Once is usually enough."

He poured some mouthwash into a cup and handed it to her, and she rinsed and spit. They went back to his bedroom, where he gave her a bottle of water and two Tylenol. She swallowed them and drank the water. "Thank you."

When they were back in bed, she murmured, voice sleepy, "I had an outstanding time tonight."

He savored the weight of her against his body. "Me too, Quinn. Me too." Caden held her, trying to forget how unnerving his reaction to her dancing with Danny had been. Sleep overtook him as he thought about how to tell her the entire story of what happened three years earlier.

He wandered through the house, looking for Mary. They'd have time to make love before they left for the New Year's Eve party. He opened the bedroom door. She was naked, wrapped in Christmas micro-lights with a man beneath her.

"What the fuck..."

"Caden, wake up! Wake up, Cade!" Quinn was shaking his shoulder. "Caden, you're dreaming!"

His eyes opened as he gulped for air. Sitting up, he ran his hands through his hair, then he felt her looking at him. "Fuck."

"What's going on?" Her hand was on his back, rubbing in circles, trying to soothe him. "You scared me."

"It's a nightmare. Did I say anything?"

"You were thrashing around. You said nothing I could understand." She looked into his eyes. "This isn't the first time, is it?"

He sighed. "No."

"Do you want to talk about it?"

"I want a drink, but that's probably not wise. Come with me." Tugging on a pair of boxers, he handed her a T-shirt and led her to the den. He grabbed two bottles of water and turned the fireplace on before motioning for her to sit on the couch.

She looked around. "This is lovely."

"It's my favorite room in the house. It calms me to be here, and I usually fall asleep." He sighed. "I can't talk about it right now."

She put her arm over his shoulder, drawing him close to her. "In the morning? Please? Let me help you carry whatever this is."

He nodded, and they watched the flames until they couldn't keep their eyes open. He stood and led her back to the bedroom, where Quinn put her arms around him and settled his head on her chest.

Chapter Two

The Aftermath

Caden

CADEN STARED AT THE bathroom mirror, trying to remember the last time he'd felt this hungover. His head was aching, even after popping some Tylenol. He'd forgotten how much alcohol was consumed at the party. Maybe Quinn being sick the night before would spare her. He hoped so.

He headed to the kitchen for coffee and drank it while looking out over the city. She came up from behind and wrapped her arms around him.

He turned to face her. She was still wearing his old Boston University T-shirt he'd given her the night before and had pulled on a pair of sweatpants. "You look cute in my shirt."

"It's a little big," she laughed. It reached almost to her knees.

"How are you feeling?"

"Shaky, and my head is pounding. I stole some Tylenol. And I'm mortified."

"Don't be." Caden admonished her.

"I haven't had someone hold my hair since my dad did when I was little. That was sweet—thank you."

Caden drew her into a hug. "At least you didn't wake up screaming like a banshee. Let's get you some coffee and then sit in the living room."

They sat down and he tucked her under his arm. "I'm sorry for the position I put you in last night. At the party." He shrugged. "And for scaring you in the middle of the night."

"The middle of the night thing..." She thought for a minute. "I didn't like seeing you so distressed. And about the party, you nailed it. Two people told me how nice it was to see you happy. Jennifer was the first, and I shut it down, then Danny. He seemed to know I was unaware of some things, and I didn't need to say anything else to him." She smiled. "I like your friends."

"They're good people."

They sat quietly for several minutes.

"Hey, Cade, I liked what we did before I so inelegantly lost my dinner. We can do that again."

He sighed. "We can definitely put that on the schedule." He tried to find the words to say what he needed to tell her, then stopped and began again. "I don't know where to start, and I'm afraid what I have to say may hurt you. It involves a long-term relationship."

She shook her head. "We're not fifteen. We both have history. Hell, you *met* my history, and I had to tell you he spent the night in my guest room. Whatever you have to say, I think I can handle it."

"Okay." He took a deep breath. "I was supposed to get married the first weekend in January three years ago. Mary and I had been together since I was twenty, and it ended on New Year's Eve. It wrecked me. That's the short version."

She drew in a breath. "I sense there's more to the story. I don't mind hearing it if you are comfortable sharing." She squeezed his hand gently. "I thought you were going to tell me you'd been married."

"Nope, just engaged. We were living in Natick, close to her job. My shift ended early on New Year's Eve, and I went home to surprise her. I found her in our bedroom having sex with some rando. I screamed at him to get the fuck out of my house, and then I went in the bathroom, where I barfed my guts out." He shook his head to dislodge the pictures of that afternoon.

"When I came out, they were both gone, and her engagement ring was on the counter. I called and texted her probably a hundred times, but she didn't respond. I took a shot of cheap whiskey, and then another and another until the bottle was empty."

He paused for a sip of coffee. Ironically, this conversation would be easier with a drink or two on board, but the thought made him ill. "We should have been at the party that night, and my friends were all calling and texting. Eventually, Danny and Brooke left and drove to Natick, looking for us. They had a key and let themselves in to find me passed out and Mary missing."

"That sounds scary for them."

"I was incoherent when they finally roused me. They were frantic. There was no sign of Mary, and I was out of it. Danny wanted to take me to the hospital." He shook his head. "We had a frat brother who almost died from alcohol poisoning, and he was worried about that. Brooke didn't want to leave because she was sure Mary would be back. And Danny didn't want to leave Brooke alone because she was eight months pregnant." What chaos it had been. "In the end, they stayed at the house and kept an eye on me."

He took a few moments before he continued. "Brooke texted Mary all night, and finally in the morning, she answered. Mary told Brooke to read her journals, and she'd understand." His hand tightened on the mug. "Mary had always journaled. I never read them. It didn't seem right. But Brooke and Danny found the journals and started reading them. It turned out she'd been screwing around for most of the time we were together." His voice broke.

Quinn turned to him. "You don't have to tell me. I feel like a voyeur peeping on something intensely personal."

"No. I want a future with you, and I feel like if that's going to happen, you need to know." Caden looked down again. "She'd given me no sign any of this was going on. It began soon after I started med school. She was alone a lot…"

"Cade." Quinn's tone was gentle but firm. "Are you excusing her behavior? Don't do that," she put her hand on his cheek. "Once is a mistake. To have it go on for years was a choice. It wasn't your fault."

"I've been working on learning that, among other things. It was hard not to wonder what I could have done differently." He swallowed. "Do you want to hear more about what a mess I was?"

Quinn nodded and took his hand.

"Danny called my parents, and they came to the house. I was still drunk and not making any sense. My dad took me to the ED—he was that concerned. I'm lucky they didn't keep me on a psych hold. Instead, they gave me anxiety meds and released me to my family. That took the edge off."

Quinn laced her fingers with his. "When did she finally come back?"

"I've never seen her again."

Quinn was speechless. "Nine years together and… I mean, you must have talked to settle things, split the assets. Nine years, and she just—disappeared?"

He nodded. "My mom and Claire took care of everything wedding-related, canceling the venue and vendors, calling all the guests, returning the gifts. They wanted me to come home with them, but I wouldn't. Danny and Robbie took turns staying with me because they didn't trust me to be alone."

"Those are some good friends."

"The best." Caden squeezed her hand and paused before continuing. "A week later, I came home from work to find her key on the counter and her clothes gone. I put the house on the market, and it sold in two weeks. I moved to my parents' condo and stayed there until I bought this place. While I was at my folks' place, I started seeing a therapist." His mug was empty now, and he headed to the kitchen for more coffee. Quinn followed him and put her arms around him while it brewed. He took a shaky breath and let her hold him before he led her back to the couch.

"Quinn, my life had been golden until that point. You asked me that first weekend if I was popular, and the answer is yes, I was. Everything came easy—friends, grades, women. I didn't have to work for any of it, and with Mary, it all collapsed like a house of cards." He rolled his shoulders. "I was nearly done with a surgical residency, and I lost the mind-set for it. I'd always been good at thinking on my feet and dealing with stressful situations, so I ended up switching to emergency medicine."

"I didn't realize you'd started out to be a surgeon."

"Yeah, I miss it sometimes, but I found a home in the ED. Being a surgeon takes a certain confidence, and I didn't have it anymore."

Caden put his arms around Quinn and buried his head against the warmth of her shoulder for several minutes. He took a deep breath and kissed her before continuing. "I told you I tried dating apps. I was a prick, angry with women, and only looking to get laid. And there were plenty of women happy with that." He sighed. "Therapy helped me realize the one-night stands, the casual sex, weren't good for me. A year ago, I gave that all up. And life's been better since then."

He laughed a little. "I wasn't looking for anyone when I saw you getting out of that car. Buying you that drink was impulsive. If I'd thought about it, I never would have done it. And then you were so easy to talk to. I don't know what my plans were at that point, but you have disrupted them."

She smiled, but it faded quickly. "I'm sorry you were treated that way. I've been hurt and lied to, but not to the point of being engaged and almost married."

Caden nodded. "One thing I need to work on is trust. You're going to have to be patient with me, please. It's why I lost my mind when you said Sam stayed in your guest room."

"I knew it pissed you off, but you're saying it was more than that?" Her eyes were steady on his.

"Yeah, way more than just pissed. Remember, we were Face Timing, and you told me I looked sweaty and pale? I was having a full-blown panic attack. My heart was racing, and I had pictures of the Natick bedroom flashing in my mind. I ended the call because I needed to get a grip on myself."

"I didn't realize it affected you so strongly." She paused. "What can I do?"

"You being brutally honest is helpful, but my issues aren't going away overnight."

"I'm brutally honest?"

He shrugged. "It was brutal hearing you had sex with Sam and had tried to rekindle things. You didn't need to tell me that. We didn't know each other when it happened. But you taking a chance, being open with me? That tells me you will be honest. You won't hide things."

She leaned into him. "I told you because I'd shared that I hadn't dated since I moved back here. I felt like that implied I hadn't had sex in that long. And truthfully, I lied about Sam when you asked about our dinner in Boston. I couldn't tell you on our first date that I'd slept with Sam or seen him after we got home. I never considered that brief time with him dating." She sighed. "I couldn't let this—our relation-ship—go forward with my lies, both spoken and unspoken, between us."

He understood that. "You can't imagine how much your openness means to me. I had a hard time last night when Danny took you out on the dance floor."

"That wasn't my idea," she murmured.

"I know. And in the past, we'd all dance with each other. It wasn't unusual for Danny to do that. It's not a rational reaction, Quinn. And I know that."

Quinn bit her lip, and Caden knew she wanted to ask something else. "You can ask me anything."

"Nine years is a long time. I'm surprised you hadn't gotten married." She shrugged. "I don't think I would have stayed in a relationship that long without marriage. I don't know." She shrugged again. "Ignore me. It's none of my business."

"I'll never ignore you." Caden kissed the top of her head. "It's a valid question. We had talked about it, but neither one of us wanted to do it while we were in school. She finished just as I started my residency. I proposed the next year and then it took us a couple of years to plan the wedding."

"Big wedding?"

"Oh yeah." Caden scoffed.

"Was the dream last night about her?"

"Yes."

"Did going to the party trigger it?"

He thought about that. "No."

"The alcohol?"

"No."

"Does it come randomly?"

"Not exactly." He leaned back against the sofa with his eyes closed. After a long pause, he said, "It's the Christmas lights."

Quinn cocked her head, and he knew she was waiting for him to elaborate.

"She had a string of white Christmas lights around her neck." Quinn drew in a sharp breath as he shook his head ruefully. "I know, huh? Pretty fucked-up. I've told no one that little tidbit, not even my therapist."

"Why not?"

"The dream didn't start until the next Christmas. I thought I'd worked everything out. And then, as soon as I saw the trees on my street wrapped in the white lights, I had the dream for the first time. It only happened once, and I kinda wrote it off. But last night was the third time this year."

"Did it happen after we went to the light show in Woodstock?"

"Yeah, that was the first time I wondered if it was fair to you to pursue this relationship."

She sat back. "Why on earth did you take me there? It must have been miserable for you."

"It wasn't." He smiled sadly. "I grabbed on to how into it you were, and I hoped it would reset something in my mind. Give me a different picture. So much for that brilliant idea."

"I wish there was something I could do."

"Me too. My therapist ought to be told about it, huh? I don't want to spend my life as a Grinch hating Christmas and everything leading up to it. I thought latching onto your enthusiasm would help. And it has. I've enjoyed this whole Christmas season with you. But the nightmare keeps hanging around."

Quinn stroked his cheek. "You've been holding a lot in."

He nodded. "I should have told you before, but every time we were together, things were so good, and I felt like admitting I lost my mind three years ago would be a real downer. Have I ruined your time here?"

She shook her head. "Not at all. I feel like I know you better now. Thank you for trusting me with it."

Caden closed his eyes and let out a sigh. "Thank *you*. How's your head?"

"Slightly better. I might survive. How about you?"

"I think I'll live too." *Time to lighten the mood.* "You know what always makes me feel better? A shower. I have an outstanding shower. You may not have noticed it when you were in the bathroom last night." He grinned at her.

She hit his arm. "Not nice picking on me. Is it big enough for two?"

"Absolutely."

Chapter Three
Revelations

Caden

AFTER THEIR SHOWER, THEY headed to Danny's house via the T. Caden suggested that after the party, a night in would be nice. They would order food, she could wear the robe, and they could make love in the living room in the glow of the city lights. Quinn smiled and nodded in agreement.

People filled every corner of Danny and Brooke's house, many the same as the night before, plus some others—including a couple of football players. "Oh my God." Quinn clutched Caden's arm and pointed at two men talking to Danny. "Those guys play for the Patriots!"

"Starstruck?" Caden laughed.

"A little, yeah."

Food was plentiful, as well as bloody Marys and mimosas. Caden gave Brooke a quick hug when she greeted them.

"There are non-alcoholic beverages in the kitchen," Brooke said. "I, for one, am not drinking alcohol today."

Quinn nodded. "Same."

While Quinn and Brooke were talking, Danny approached Caden. "Hey, I hear me dancing with Quinn triggered something for you. I'm sorry. Never gave a thought to how that might affect you."

"I hoped that would stay between Brooke and me. It's not your fault I'm a head case. And I heard you thought it was nice seeing me happy."

Danny smiled. "Well, yeah. I like her. Did she like us, or did we overwhelm her?"

"She had a good time and drank too much, as we always do. We had a long talk this morning. I told her all about Mary."

"Way to start out the year. I imagine that was tough for you."

"Oh yeah. But I'm glad it's out in the open."

They stayed until midafternoon, watching football. Danny told Caden about a hockey game in the morning, and Caden said he'd try to make it. Before they left, Danny said they should get together again, just the four of them.

When they left, Caden took Quinn to explore the Back Bay. They spent a couple of hours walking on little side streets she'd never seen before. He knew she'd always seen Boston through a tourist's eyes, and he enjoyed letting her see it as a native. Many of the houses featured window boxes filled with evergreen, or cedar branches, and pinecones. Ribbons wound around the branches, ending in enormous bows. On one street, all the window boxes matched.

"I love this," she gushed. "All the decorations seem to be coordinated. They are exquisite and very different from the random decor people near me put up. And I love the cobblestone streets."

Caden drew her closer. It was almost twilight when they popped out of a side street onto Beacon Street, near the Massachusetts State House. They stood for a few minutes looking down at Boston Common as the adjacent buildings twinkled with lights.

"I've never been to this area in the winter. It's so pretty." Quinn turned to face him. "I'm sorry that you don't enjoy the lights as much as I do."

"I know. Give me time, I'll get there. I love watching your delight." They started walking and were standing at the steps to the brownstone when Caden asked, "Would you be willing to walk down to the waterfront? Or is that too far?"

"Caden, I climb mountains. We'll call it urban hiking. Are we going to eat down there?"

"No." He told her about the Medico van. "One guy, Ned, had an infected cut when I was there the day after Christmas. I went back on my own, on Monday and he was doing okay, but I'd like to check on him again. You don't have to come. It can be rough at the encampment."

"I want to go. I want to know all about your life."

They went inside and while Caden filled a backpack, Quinn investigated the kitchen. She ran her hand over the quartz countertop on the island. The light color was in stark contrast to the shaker style, dark espresso cabinets. "Your kitchen is amazing. Brooke said you gave her an unlimited budget."

"Pretty much. The building deserved the best."

"Hey Doc," Marty greeted them. "I'm glad you came. Ned hasn't come out of his tent in two days."

"Damn," Caden muttered under his breath. "That's what I was afraid of." He pushed aside the flap of the tent, where Ned was lying wrapped in blankets. The fetid odor that permeated the camp was even stronger in the tent.

Quinn was close behind him and Caden waved her away, but she ignored him. "How can I help?"

"Call 911. He's got to go to the hospital." Caden swung his backpack onto the ground and kneeled beside Ned. He took his temperature and pulse. "Jesus. Ned, we've called an ambulance. You don't have a choice now. You're going to the hospital."

The prone man said nothing, only moaned in response. His body was shaking with chills.

When the paramedics arrived, Caden moved out of the way, "Hey, Cade." Alan had been with him in the van the day after Christmas. "Did you call this in? I thought they said the call came from a woman."

Caden put his arm over Quinn's shoulder. "This is Quinn Michaels. I asked her to call it in as soon as I saw how bad he was." Alan flashed him a knowing smile before joining his partner, and Caden realized how good it felt to introduce Quinn.

Ned was still on the ground when the shaking that Caden had seen grew stronger. "He's seizing," Alan exclaimed.

Caden and Quinn stayed out of the way until Alan said, "We're going to have to intubate, we could use an extra pair of hands, Cade."

"Quinn's a nurse if you need her," Caden said as he followed Alan's directions.

Within minutes of the seizure stopping, they lifted Ned onto a stretcher, then loaded him into the ambulance. Caden said, "I'll call and let them know you're en route." After he finished the call, he turned to Quinn. "Wait here for a second." He walked over to the group. They had watched intently as the paramedics and Caden worked on Ned.

One of the women spoke first. "Is he going to be okay, Doc?"

"I honestly don't know." He looked directly at Marty as he admonished the group. "Don't let it get that bad again."

Marty responded as Caden turned back toward Quinn. "Thanks for coming Cade."

When Caden reached her, Quinn took his hand and said, "You saved his life. If we hadn't come...he would have died in that tent. You're so calm and focused. I see why you work in the Emergency Department."

Caden brought her hand to his chest on top of his pounding heartbeat. "Calm on the outside, maybe, but that was way too close. Let's head home."

As they settled in for the evening, Quinn said, "I want to call my parents to wish them a Happy New Year."

"Why don't you FaceTime?" Caden was standing at the kitchen counter. "Then you can introduce me."

Her mom answered right away, and Quinn showed her some of the brownstone, the high ceilings, the woodwork, and the view of the city lights. Caden patted the couch next to him to let her know he wanted her to sit down and let him join the conversation. Her face broke into a wide smile as she settled onto the couch and brought him into the frame. "Is Dad nearby?"

"Right behind me." Her father appeared on the phone screen.

"Dad, Mom, this is Caden Brady." She moved the phone to showcase Caden's face. "Cade, this is my parents, Hank and Mel Michaels."

Her mom spoke first. "It's nice to meet you, Caden. You have a beautiful home."

"Thank you. Quinn and I found we share an affinity for historic buildings. I'm happy to meet you and Mr. Michaels."

"Hank and Mel." Quinn's father's voice was decisive. "We don't want to feel like we're back in school." Everyone laughed, then her mother asked how the party was.

"It was so much fun. Not like anything I'd ever been to. Everyone wore beautiful clothes, and we danced until midnight." Quinn put her hand on Caden's thigh. "I drank too much."

Her mother shook her head, grinning. "You threw up, didn't you?"

Caden chuckled. "A regular occurrence?"

Quinn rolled her eyes. "Thanks, Mom. On a happier topic, we've firmed up our plans for next weekend. We'll come up on Friday night and stay until Sunday. I've reserved a room at the hotel." Her mother protested, but Quinn stayed firm.

"Do they not know how stubborn you are?" Caden posed the question with a smile on his face and told Mel about the snowstorm before Christmas when Quinn had insisted he drive her car back to Boston.

Her dad came back into the frame and asked, "Are you going to have time to go for a couple of runs down the mountain with me, Quinny?"

"That's high on my agenda, Dad."

The conversation ended with Quinn telling them she would be in touch during the week.

They ordered food, and while they were waiting for the delivery, Quinn said, "I have an awkward question."

"Ask me anything." God knew he had few secrets left.

"How do you afford a place like this? I know you said you had a place in Natick, so you must have had a down payment from that, but there's a big difference between Natick and the Back Bay. And you must have student loans?"

Caden was standing at the window, watching for the food delivery. He sighed before answering. "My grandfather was a contractor. He started out as a laborer and worked his way up until he had his own company. The company was successful, very successful." He paused. "When I was twenty-two, there was an accident on a construction site. He died along with three of his employees."

Quinn drew in a sharp breath, but Caden continued talking before she could say anything. "I told you this morning my life had been golden. Losing Gramps was the one part of it that wasn't. My grandmother had died two years earlier, and my dad was an only child. So, his entire estate went to my family. He had set up trust funds for me and my sisters. And then it turned out faulty steel caused the accident. It took a few years, but there was a very large settlement, which increased the amount of our trust funds. I gained access to a lot of money when I turned twenty-five, an obscene amount of money."

It was a lot for her to process, but it was good to tell her. Caden turned to look at Quinn.

There were tears in her eyes as she gazed at him. "I'm sorry about your grandfather. I don't have any experience with something like that, but I've always thought when I read about big settlements, they don't make up for losing someone you loved."

He nodded. "Yes, exactly. My grandparents lived next door to us when we were growing up. They were a huge part of our lives. I feel blessed that I had twenty-two years with him. Chrissy was only five when Gram died and seven when Gramps died. She hardly knew them."

Quinn put her arms around him. "So, you're…"

Caden put his hand gently over her mouth. "Don't say it." He moved his hand, and she grasped it. "Yes, I'm rich. No student loans."

She nodded. "And it's how you bought the house in Natick and why you didn't have to split the assets with Mary."

"Yes."

Quinn was silent for a bit before she asked, "Is the money the reason Mary stayed with you?"

He winced, but nodded. "That's the prevailing opinion."

"That sucks."

"Yeah, it does." He heaved an enormous sigh. "Now you know my two biggest secrets. How I lost my mind three years ago and that I have a trust fund."

Quinn shook her head, looking baffled. "You act like having money is a problem."

"It colors my relationships."

"Has it changed your relationship with Danny and Robbie? You said you've known them since high school or longer."

"No, they treat me the same. Truthfully, they give me shit about it."

"You started dating Mary as a poor college schlub, and then a couple years in, you became a trust fund baby. So, you don't know if she stayed because she loved you or for the money. Yeah, I'd agree that the money colored that relationship."

Caden admired her ability to cut to the chase. "There you go with that brutal honesty."

"And now you're not sure of me."

He gazed into her eyes, unsure of how to respond. She gave great clarity to his jumbled thoughts about the money.

She put her hands on his cheeks. "You're a doctor, and doctors have money. I knew that within minutes of you handing me that chai. The first time we texted, you told me you owned a brownstone in the Back Bay. I knew that didn't come cheaply. The first time we went out, I discovered you drive a BMW, not the car of a pauper. I've known from the beginning you must have money, but it's not why I'm here. You're going to have to trust me on that."

"I know. Man, this has been an emotional day. Grueling." He sighed again, and Quinn wrapped her arms around him, seeking his mouth. He had laid himself bare, and her touch and kisses brought him comfort.

True to his word, Caden made sure they did more of what they had done the night before as the city lights glowed in the distance.

Chapter Four

Brooke Has Reservations

Quinn

THEY LEFT THE BROWNSTONE midmorning, and Caden skated into the hockey game in the second period. Brooke was there with her son, and Quinn sat with them. Brooke was quieter than she had been on New Year's Eve, and Quinn searched for something to talk about. "Do you come to all the games?"

"No, just a few here and there. I thought you'd be here, and I wanted to talk to you." Brooke turned to face her. "Caden is the best man I know."

"He's amazing," Quinn agreed. She studied Brooke's face. "Wait. Is something wrong?"

"He went through hell with Mary. I don't want to see him hurt again."

"Neither do I. I know we haven't known each other long, but he's the most incredible man I've ever met." Quinn's body flushed with heat. *She doesn't like me. What did I do? We really hit it off at the dinner dance.*

"Cade told me you let your ex sleep in your guest room."

"I-I..." *I did nothing wrong, Caden knows that. I don't know why he told her about Sam staying at my townhouse, but someone I barely know will not intimidate me.* Quinn took a deep breath. "My relationship with Sam ended ten years ago. We had a brief reunion in the fall, but it was completely over when Caden texted me for the first time. I was looking out for a friend when Sam stayed in my guest room. Cade knows all that." She concentrated on watching the play on the ice.

Several minutes passed and Quinn finally asked, "Why did he tell you about that?" *It was a private moment between us. I didn't expect him to tell anyone.*

"He had a panic attack when you danced with Danny."

"Dancing with your husband wasn't my idea." Quinn had a hard time keeping the anger she was feeling out of her voice.

"I knew something was wrong and when I asked, he told me what was going on and that it wasn't the first time."

Quinn took several deep breaths. "I appreciate that Caden has good friends who watch out for him. I have the same, and they mean the world to me." She paused. "I hope you'll all be able to accept me as a part of his life."

"It's going to take some time. We were all burned by Mary."

"Did you like her?"

Brooke sighed. "Yes. And if she walked up to us now, I'd scratch her eyes out." She rolled her eyes. "It's not like me to feel such deep hatred for someone."

"I'll consider myself warned. 'Cross Brooke and risk my eyesight.' Do I have that right?"

"More or less." Brooke looked out on the ice. "He's happier than we've seen him in a long time."

"So am I." Quinn watched the action on the ice and when Danny passed the puck to Caden who slid it around a defenseman and into the goal, she cheered along with Brooke. Caden dropped to one knee and pumped his arm, then found Quinn in the stands and winked at her.

After a few more minutes of concentrating on the ice, Quinn said, "Can I ask you what Mary was like?"

"She was charming, cultured and very sure of herself. Also, sneaky, manipulative and dishonest. Sadly, she kept those last three traits hidden until the end."

"Would she have been here today?"

"No. She came to his games in the beginning, but once she was sure of her place in his life, she stopped. She wasn't into sports at all. Looking back at it now, we see all the signs that she wasn't a good match."

"Was Cade that dazzled by her? I'll confess, I'm intimidated because he was so in love with someone for such a long time."

"In the beginning, yes. She was beautiful, she said and did all the right things during his last two years of college. Then he started Med School, and he was too busy to notice that the relationship was deteriorating. Mary was from Philadelphia, and she started going home more often. At least, that is what she said she was doing. When Danny and I read her journals that terrible morning, we found out that on some of those 'trips', she was actually staying with other men, sometimes right here in Boston." Brooke had been watching the ice, then she turned to Quinn. "That probably makes Caden seem clueless, but he wasn't. School consumed him, and then his residency. She did all the right things to make him believe she loved him. Did he tell you about his grandfather getting killed?"

Quinn nodded. "Yes, last night. It sounds like it had a profound effect on him."

"It did. His whole family was lost for a while. And for sure, that's why Mary stayed around. The allure of all that money was too much for her to walk away from. As soon as his inheritance came through, she started lobbying for a proposal, and then for him to buy that house in Natick. I think if they'd gotten married, she would have divorced him within a year or two and tried to get a big fat settlement. Maybe she would have waited until they had a kid. That way, she could have gotten even more. She had us all fooled, though."

"False friends. I've had a few of those." Quinn thought about her friend Julie and how she had betrayed her more than once. "I understand your reluctance about me. I'm cautious about who I elevate to friend status. My feelings for Caden came out of the blue. I hadn't even been on a date in two years."

The game ended with Caden's team winning. He and Danny swapped their hockey jerseys for dry shirts, collected their gear, and started walking toward the women.

"He's going to be pissed at me for being protective of him." Brooke grinned. "Because you're going to tell him about this conversation, aren't you?"

"Yes, I learned the hard way about keeping secrets. I hope you'll learn that what you see is what you get with me."

"And you'll forgive me for being blunt?"

Quinn nodded just as Caden and Danny reached them. Caden wrapped his arms around Quinn, holding her while Danny lifted his son Liam, and leaned over to kiss Brooke. "Didn't know how that game was going to go with Robbie off doing his guardian ad litem work."

Caden chuckled. "It's going to kill him to realize we can win without him. Let's get some lunch."

They stopped at a nearby pub, and with the men there, the tension between Quinn and Brooke eased. When they finished,

Caden led her toward Boston Common. "Is there a place to rent skates near the Frog Pond?"

"Yes, don't worry about that."

"Liam really likes you." Quinn said.

"The feeling is mutual. Brooke and Danny were the first of my friends to have kids. I'm his godfather."

"Oh, that's sweet. What about Robbie and Jennifer?"

"They're trying, but nothing yet. I hope it happens soon for them. Jen was made to be a mom."

When they arrived at the Frog Pond, Caden pulled a pair of white figure skates out of his bag. "You're expecting this to be a regular thing, huh?" Quinn looked at him with a smile.

His eyes sparkled at her as he nodded. She was steadier this time when she started out, and they skated a little faster and a little longer. After a couple of hours on the ice, they headed back toward the brownstone, stopping at a cafe on Newbury Street for a warm drink.

"Brooke thinks I can't be trusted because of Sam staying in my guest room before Christmas."

Caden's face contorted, and he exhaled heavily. "I told her on New Year's Eve about the first panic attack." He reached for her hand. "I'm sorry. What else did she say?"

"The gist of it was that it will not be easy for her to accept me because of how Mary fooled her. I'll confess, it was disconcerting. I understand how she feels. It was just hard feeling like she didn't like me."

"Oh babe, thank you for telling me. I'll talk to her."

Quinn shook her head. "No. Don't do that. We came to an understanding. I'm not going to hide things from you, Cade. You mean too much to me."

"I feel the same way."

After showering, they headed to the waterfront for dinner with Caden's family. Despite having met Claire and James, Quinn was nervous. His parents were a different story. As they walked out of the subway stop, Caden said, "My sister Cathleen's hair is pink."

Quinn turned to look at him. "Do you have a problem with that?"

"No. But it was a surprise when I walked into the house on Christmas morning."

"Probably good you didn't meet me in my green hair phase."

"Green? Really? When was that?"

"About six months after I graduated from college. My life had gone to hell, and I needed a diversion. I had various colors over a couple of years."

"Maybe that's what it is for Cath. I think something is bothering her. We're going to have dinner next week." Caden led her to the door to his parent's building and while she tried to calm her nerves, Caden pressed the keypad and drummed his fingers on the wall. "It always takes them forever to let me in, even when they know I'm coming." He shook his head, looking exasperated.

Quinn put her hand over his. "You're nervous too."

He grinned ruefully as the door buzzed to let them in. "A little."

His mother opened the penthouse door before Caden could knock, so he took the initiative. "Ma, this is Quinn Michaels. Quinn, my mom, Maureen."

Quinn opened her mouth, but before she could get any words out, Maureen gathered her into a hug. "I'm so happy to meet you. We're huggers. Hope you don't mind."

She laughed. "Claire told me the same thing. I'm getting used to it." Already, the Brady family was putting her at ease.

Maureen led her toward the kitchen. "Cade, your father's in the living room watching a football game, why don't you join him. Quinn can keep me company while I put the finishing touches on dinner."

Caden looked nervously at Quinn as she nodded to let him know she'd be fine.

"So," Maureen began, "you live near Claire?"

"I do. And we work at the same hospital—of course, in totally different areas. Such a small world."

"It sure is. Did you grow up in Hanover?"

"No, I'm from a small town about an hour north, across the border in Vermont."

"Have you been at Dartmouth long?"

"Ma!" Caden called from the living room. "Stop with the third degree!"

"It's fine, Cade," Quinn called back. Turning back to his mother, she said, "I've been there a couple of years."

Maureen shook her head. "I'm sorry. I don't mean to pry, but he hasn't told us anything about you. He's probably told you I'm too nosy."

Before Quinn could say anything, Caden's sisters came in, and Maureen introduced them.

Oh god, Quinn thought, *how am I going to remember who is who?*

Cathleen smiled reassuringly. "I'm Cathleen, and I'm the one with pink hair, if you're trying to keep track. I'm the only one who has my mom's coloring. Minus my current hair color, of course."

Quinn noted the light-brown roots and hazel eyes Cathleen shared with her mother. "You live in North Carolina?"

"Oh no, Cade has talked about me." Cathleen grinned. "I thought moving a thousand miles away would prevent that."

Chloe and Chrissy had dark hair like Caden, although not as curly, and the same blue eyes. Quinn could see they got their coloring from their father, a handsome man in his mid-fifties.

They all helped put the food on the table, and as they sat down, Maureen asked, "Do you have siblings, Quinn?"

Caden glared at his mother, and Quinn put her hand on his leg. "No, I'm an only child."

Chloe sighed. "Oh, how wonderful that would be." The other girls nodded in agreement, while Caden shrugged.

Chrissy scoffed at him. "Yeah, you wouldn't agree. You were the prince. You do not know what it's like following three older sisters and you, the golden child!"

He snorted. "It's no picnic putting up with the four of you, either. Chrissy, did you get all your college applications in?" He turned to Quinn. "Mom and Dad completely dropped the reins after getting through four of us, so I have to keep on her to get anything done."

Sean and Maureen looked at each other, rolling their eyes.

Chrissy tore off a piece of bread and threw it at him. "I guess you finally figured out your orientation, huh? I was a little worried about you back in November."

Caden looked at the ceiling, shaking his head. "Don't try to get a job in my emergency department. I don't like your mean streak."

"As if I would!"

Everyone at the table was laughing, and even as a newcomer, Quinn recognized the good-natured ribbing. It showed her a different side of Caden, one she enjoyed.

In a blatant effort to get the discussion under control, Maureen asked how they had spent the day. Caden answered, "I played hockey this morning, and then we went skating at the Frog Pond."

"I'm a skier, not a skater," Quinn admitted. "He's teaching me."

Chloe shook her head. "Don't let him dress you up in pads..."

Caden held up his hand, interrupting her. "Don't you say it!"

"And put you in the goal while he takes shots at you," Chloe finished, sticking her tongue out at Caden.

Laughter bubbled up inside Quinn. "Oh my God, Claire said the exact same thing."

Caden shrugged again. "I had to have someone to protect the goal. For the record, you girls all sucked as goalies!" He looked at Quinn. "I promise I will never shoot pucks at you."

They spent over two hours with his family, and as they were leaving, Maureen asked when Quinn was coming to Boston again.

Quinn smiled. "I'm taking him to Vermont next weekend to meet my parents, and then I'll be here the weekend after because we're going to a playoff game." She looked at Caden for confirmation, and he nodded.

"Why don't you come for lunch on Sunday? We can eat around noon."

"We can do that." Caden smiled at his mother.

Maureen hugged Quinn, then turned to him. Quinn heard her whisper in his ear as she hugged him. "I tried to restrain myself."

He chuckled and whispered back, "It's all good."

Once they were outside, Quinn laughed. "Is it like that every time you get together?"

He nodded. "More or less. Did it scare you off?"

"Not at all. It was a little overwhelming, but I loved it."

When they reached the brownstone, Caden started to help Quinn off with her coat and then paused. "There's something I want to show you." At the end of the hallway, he opened a door that revealed a stairway Quinn had not seen. With a smile, Caden led her up the stairs where another door waited. He opened it, then they stepped out onto a rooftop terrace.

Quinn gasped as she saw the view. Caden reached for a switch on the wall and Edison bulbs flooded the space with light. She swiveled her head to take in everything. A large teak table surrounded by padded chairs anchored the space. There was an outdoor kitchen along one side and on the opposite side was a conversation area with a couch and two chairs. Wrought iron fencing shielded a long, open expanse of the roof. "This is a beautiful space, Cade. Even better than the terrace off your living room."

"I knew you'd like it." He slung his arm over her shoulder. "Want to sit for a bit? Or is it too cold?"

"I'd love to sit." She walked toward the couch. "We'll keep each other warm. Do you spend much time up here?"

"Not really. I have dinner parties up here in the summer, but don't come up here by myself very often."

Quinn knew it was his height phobia that kept him away. "Who do you share this amazing space with?"

"My family, Danny, Robbie and the girls, some doctors I'm friends with. Last year we had our end of season hockey party up here." Caden grimaced. "That won't happen again. Drunk hockey players on a roof. Not a good combination. Even with the amount of alcohol I had, I was still climbing out of my skin that one of them would topple off. I was ecstatic when that night ended." He grinned at her.

"Hockey players are big drinkers?"

"Some more than others." Caden pulled her close, moving her legs over his lap. "This is nice."

Quinn nodded. "Do you cook or cater for these dinner parties?"

"Depends on who's here. I'm good at grilling. If it's my family, my mother insists on helping, surprise, surprise. With the doctors, I have it catered because I want to be fully engaged."

"I can't wait to see you on the grill."

"This summer. We'll cook together." They sat for a few minutes with the only sound being traffic on the road below. Caden lowered his lips to hers and then said, "You *are* cold. We should go downstairs, but first, come here." He stood, took her hand, and led her to the railing. He put his arm over her shoulder, pulling her close. "Do you recognize any of the buildings?"

"Some, like the Prudential Center."

With his free hand, Caden pointed out some spots he thought Quinn would be familiar with. "There's a plane coming in for a landing," he said, pointing at the sky and then moving his hand, "and one taking off."

"Do you like to travel? We haven't talked much about that."

"I haven't done a lot. Five kids didn't lend itself to long trips. We went to Disney World once, but that was before Chrissy was born. I did a spring break trip to Miami with some of the guys." He rolled his eyes at Quinn. "If you grew up in a Hallmark movie, that trip hit every stereotype in the book."

"Just one spring break?"

"Yeah, I got busy with other things, then med school and my residency. I fail miserably at work life balance. These weekends I've had with you are the most time I've taken for myself in years."

"I like to travel. I hope you'll want to do that with me."

"The longest and best trip I ever took was to Ireland with my dad and my grandfather. Traveling with you will be even more amazing. I can't wait to explore the world with you." Then he leaned down and nuzzled her neck. "You bring me such serenity."

Quinn sighed and arched against him. Caden brought his other arm around her and said, "Except for those many moments that I'm a burning ball of desire for you." He feathered kisses along her jawbone. "Like now. We should go downstairs so we can warm each other up."

Chapter Five

Exploration

Quinn

ON SUNDAY MORNING, QUINN dressed in the brown suede leggings and oatmeal-colored sweater she was wearing the day they met. When she came out of the guest room, Caden leered and put his arms around her, reaching his hands down to her butt. "Yup, this is exactly what I was thinking about as you stood outside that building."

A rideshare dropped them off outside of a hotel with a rooftop restaurant. She looked at him with a question in her eyes.

"Yes," Caden said, "we're eating on the top floor."

Quinn squealed and grabbed his face with both hands. "Did you know I've always wanted to eat here?"

"It seemed likely since you like being up high and you like looking at the city."

They took the elevator to the twenty-ninth floor. The doors opened to a panoramic view of the city. The hostess led them to a corner table next to the window. In one direction, they could look at the city and in the other, they could see the harbor. Quinn looked at Caden with concern. "Are you okay? I'd be fine sitting farther away from the glass if you aren't comfortable."

He shook his head. "I asked for this table. I'm logical enough to know the glass will not melt away, opening us up to danger."

Quinn had eggs benedict, Caden a Belgian waffle, and they both had mimosas. "We need to talk about our schedules for January. I have to work the weekend after the football game, then two weeks later I go to Maine for my classes."

"I'm on that weekend between you working and going to Maine." Caden frowned. "I don't like the idea of going three weeks without seeing you. Maybe we can meet in southern New Hampshire for dinner."

Quinn took a sip of her mimosa. "I like that idea." *It will all be fine.*

Back at the brownstone, Quinn told Caden she needed to leave soon.

Caden led her to the bedroom and reached for the hem of her sweater. When she nodded, he gently pulled it off. His hands ran up and down her back and sides before moving her bra out of the way to get to her breasts.

She lowered his zipper and slipped her hand inside to stroke his erection through his boxers.

"Let's make this last," he murmured.

Quinn nodded. They'd had plenty of passion-crazed encounters this weekend, so taking their time to enjoy each other would be nice.

Nudging her to sit on the bed, he kneeled to remove her boots. He started rubbing her feet, and her body twitched in response, trying to feed the fire between her legs. "I love the way you squirm when I do this."

"Mmm. You wouldn't believe what it does to me."

"I'm pretty sure I would." One hand moved up her leg and stroked her center before he went back to her feet.

"I feel like I'm not contributing anything."

"Keep squirming. You're contributing plenty." Eventually, he unzipped her pants and slid them off.

Caden stood, and Quinn pushed his pants to the floor, along with his boxers. She unbuttoned his shirt, flicked his nipples, and leaned forward to take one between her teeth. He moaned and pushed toward her. She took his cock in her mouth and cradled his balls.

He moaned. "Oh God, you know what that does to me. This won't make it last." She reluctantly shifted away, and he took her in his arms. "I want to look at all of you. I want to know any freckles or moles you have in private places."

Caden unhooked her bra, making them both naked, and nuzzled her neck. "I love your scent. The citrus makes me think of walking through an orange grove with you in the sunshine. I can't wait until we go to Florida in March." They had bought their airline tickets on Friday night.

His lips traced from her neck down her front until he reached her breasts. Taking one in his mouth, he swirled his tongue around her nipple. She moaned in response, and he moved away, gently stroking her while he explored her skin.

"I bet you look even more gorgeous with the hint of a tan. I'll finally get to see you in those bathing suits you've sent me pictures of. Such a tease." His voice was husky with desire.

Moaning again, she pulled him back toward her breast.

"No, no, I'm not finished looking yet." His hands glided down to her belly and over her hips. "I love your curves and your skin, so soft and so perfect." She writhed under his touch. His fingers moved gently between her legs. "Aha! You have a mole on your inner thigh. I hadn't noticed that before."

Quinn couldn't stop moving against his touch. "You are killing me!"

"I love the way you respond to my touch. The squirms and the thrusting... you turn me on so much." Caden continued to stroke her clit and looked toward her legs. Sliding off the bed, he took one of her feet in his hands again. "God, you've made me into such a pervert. I never had any fetishes before."

Quinn slid off the bed until she was sitting next to him on the floor. Her arms went around him as her lips sought his. He teasingly resisted her tongue as it pressed to his lips, trying to get into his mouth, until she finally won and was welcomed in.

Tearing herself away from his mouth, she announced, "Now it's my turn." She tugged him onto the bed.

Her hands lingered on his legs and she felt Caden watching as she studied him.

"What's this scar on your knee?" she asked. "Did you have stitches?"

"Fell on some rocks at the beach. Took five stitches to close it."

She kissed the scar and licked it before continuing up his body.

He moaned and pushed toward her. She fluttered kisses up his thigh, being extra careful not to touch his very hard cock. "Now you're really teasing me. I have body parts needing attention."

"All in good time. I'm paying you back." She licked between his legs and moved her hands to his butt, letting her fingers move to places they hadn't been before. He jerked at her touch and lifted on his elbows, giving her a quizzical look. She cocked her head. "Do you like that?"

Caden sighed, a little shakily. "Possibly."

"I'll have to remember that." She continued to play, enjoying his response. His abs received her attention next as she kissed and stroked them. "Your body is amazing." Moving to his nipples, she traced circles around them before lowering her mouth to suck on one.

His voice thick with desire, he moaned, "God, Quinn, you're destroying me. I think we're even now."

She stretched out beside him and started stroking his cock. "Is this the body part you were talking about? The one that needs attention?"

"Yeah." Reaching one hand down to her clit, which was dripping wet, he played gently and then pushed two fingers inside her. He stroked them in and out as she groaned and moved against him.

"I am so turned-on," she breathed, "but I want you inside me."

Caden withdrew his fingers and brought them to his mouth, licking them before kissing her.

She sheathed him with a condom before climbing on top and lowering herself onto him, going slowly until he was fully inside. She stopped and stared into Caden's eyes.

His gaze met hers, and he whispered, "Oh, babe."

They stayed still, relishing their connection, until Caden pushed up on his forearms to reach Quinn's breasts. He teased the nipple with his tongue, and she started moving her hips in time with his, their passion growing until they climaxed wordlessly together.

Tears flooded Quinn's eyes as she looked down at his face. "I love you. It's overwhelming. I don't expect anything..."

Caden put a finger over her lips and with his other hand brushed the tears away. "My feelings for you are more than I ever thought I'd let myself have again." He held her until their breathing returned to normal, then went to the bathroom. After coming back, he wrapped his arms around her. "I don't want you to leave. I can't remember when I've enjoyed welcoming in a new year more."

She laid her head on his shoulder. "I feel the same way. But it's just a week until we head to Vermont."

Chapter Six

Cathleen Confides

Caden

CADEN ROSE FROM HIS chair when he saw Cathleen enter O'Malley's. He pulled her chair out before wrapping his arms around his sister in a quick hug.

"You've still got those manners." Cathleen grinned at him as she shrugged off her coat and unwound a brightly colored scarf. "It's cold here." She shivered. "I'm not used to this." She had been living in North Carolina since she started college. Six years later, she was just one semester away from a master's degree in counseling.

"And yet, you're thinking about moving back here."

"Not just thinking about." Cathleen's eyes were bright with excitement. "I landed a gig as an intern to the school counselor at The Jefferson School in Enfield. She's a year or two from retirement. I'll accumulate the clinical hours I need and hopefully move into the counselor role when she leaves." The town she named was a short distance from Hanover. "The Head of School called with the offer this afternoon. I'm looking forward to being done with school."

Caden raised his eyebrows.

"Okay, you're right. I'll still be at a school, but I won't be a student anymore. I'm looking forward to that."

"Congratulations." He extended his fist in congratulations. "It feels good to nail down that first job after college." A server approached their table, and Caden ordered two shots of Irish Whiskey. "I didn't realize you were thinking about school counseling."

"I wasn't. But I did an internship last semester at a high school, and I had a couple of kids that I know I made a difference in their lives. That was a good feeling, so I started looking at what was available. I don't have to do it forever if I don't like it." Cathleen looked thoughtfully at her older brother. "Kinda like you and the Emergency Department." He'd been vocal when he started at Mass General that he might not stay.

"And look at me now, over two years in," Caden said as the server placed their drinks on the table. He lifted his glass and tapped it against Cathleen's. "To new beginnings. It'll be fun to have you closer. And I'm sure Mom is delighted." His grin was devilish.

"Don't remind me." Cathleen groaned. "This is terrible, but I didn't even tell her I had the interview last week and I swore Claire to secrecy. I haven't told her I'm coming back. You're the first." Their mother was well known for being overly involved in her children's lives. "Mom is the reason I didn't apply for anything in Boston. There were a lot of desirable positions, but I can't be in the same city. I don't know how you and Chloe do it."

"Did Claire tell you about me asking Mom to stay out of my life before Christmas?"

"She did. I would love to have been there." Her eyes twinkled at him again. "Now that you've brought it up, looks like you have your own new beginnings going on."

"I do." A server came to take their order and as he walked away, Caden asked, "I suppose you all dissected her six ways to Sunday after we left."

Cathleen looked chagrined as she said, "Maybe. I know people who repeat the same pattern over and over, especially in looks. You certainly haven't done that. Quinn couldn't look any less like Mary."

"She's nothing like Mary and not just physically. Her interests are different, and her upbringing was middle class, much like ours." When Cathleen rolled her eyes, Caden paused. "I grew up middle class. That money from Gramps didn't come into play until I was done with college." He played with the label on his empty beer bottle. "I told Quinn about the money. God, I hated having to do that."

"I know. We're probably the only five siblings in the world who have issues with having money rather than the opposite. I've told no one in North Carolina that I will get copious amounts of money when I turn twenty-five." The server slid a plate in front of her. "To return to our dissection of your new girlfriend. I liked her. We all did. She was quiet, but she held her own."

Caden smiled. "I like her too, a lot." The same feeling that he'd had on Friday night when the paramedics saw him with Quinn flowed over him. *God, that feels so good.*

"It hasn't been that long, has it? Mom wasn't sure."

"We met two months ago today." Caden had awoken thinking about the date and had flowers delivered to Quinn. "I don't think there's an arbitrary timeline on falling in love."

"Love, huh? Does she feel the same way?"

"She does. I'm having a hard time articulating it to her." Caden let the food on his plate occupy his attention for a few minutes, and then he looked back at his sister. "Do you remember that wooden box with the Celtic knot that you and Claire argued over the day you all helped me clean out the Natick house?"

She nodded. "Claire wanted to kill me over that. What was in it?"

"It was filled with things from my time with Mary. Ticket stubs, programs, a poker chip, a baseball, you know the kind of stuff. I jammed it in my closet when I moved into the brownstone, and it's been there ever since. I dug it out on Christmas night and went through it. Then I got rid of it. Threw it in a fire at a homeless encampment."

"What about the engagement ring? Claire seemed to think you still have that."

"I did. I don't now." His face was stern, leaving no room for Cathleen to question him. Caden let the food distract him again, and she did the same.

"Throwing that bag of crap into a fire was one of the most satisfying things I've done in a long time. I literally felt like a weight dropped off my heart." Caden pushed his empty plate away and ordered two more beers when the server came to the table. "I didn't ask you to dinner to talk about me. What's going on with you?"

Cathleen took a sip of the beer, and then a deep breath. "Let's throw some darts." She pushed back her chair and walked to the dartboard. "Red or blue?" She held the darts out to him.

Caden took red and gave her a look that acknowledged her avoidance of personal talk. Cathleen took great pleasure in beating him in the first game, and he insisted on another one. "I'd forgotten how competitive you could be."

Cathleen had been state champion in the one ten hurdles her senior year in high school. "It's never a good idea to underestimate me. Wasn't in high school, and it still isn't." She threw a bullseye to open the second game and beat him by ten points.

"Don't tell Danny and Rob. I'll lose my street cred."

"Can't admit you lost to a girl." Cathleen smirked, then her face grew serious. "Can we go to your house? I don't want to talk here."

Caden agreed, and they bundled into their coats for the short walk to his brownstone. He opened the door and led her toward the back of the building. "You haven't seen the gym I put in."

Cathleen inspected each piece of equipment. "Top shelf. I'd expect nothing less." She grinned at him. "Can I come over to work out while I'm here?"

"Of course." He shared the code to get in while they walked up to the second floor. "You want another beer?" Caden walked to the kitchen and returned with two bottles.

Cathleen made herself comfortable on the couch, took a swallow of the beer and asked, "What do you want to talk about?"

"Why you're really coming home. You said there's nothing holding you in North Carolina anymore. It sounded like there was more to the story."

She shook her head.

"Don't give me that, Cath. You can't hide your emotions any better than the rest of us, and you looked sad when we talked on Christmas Day. Maybe even more than sad. I thought you had a boyfriend."

"I did. His name was Larken. A true southerner, he's lived his whole life in North Carolina. I met him on the rowing team." She stopped and let her eyes meet Caden's. "You know I'm doing crew, don't you?"

Caden looked embarrassed. "Mom may have mentioned something, but it's such an info dump when I go over for dinner that I tune a lot out. I'm sorry. I've really lost touch with you."

Cathleen shrugged. "It goes both ways. I joined this team when I started grad school. Lark started the next summer, and we hit it off. He asked me out and after a while, we just kind of became a couple."

"Was it serious?" Caden wasn't aware of any serious relationships for her.

"We agreed to be exclusive. We slept together...he wanted me to move in with him, but I hadn't."

"I sense I'm not the only one who has a hard time articulating what I feel."

"It's not that I have a hard time saying it. What I felt for him wasn't what I imagined being in love would feel like." She took a drink. "I mean, we had fun, the sex was okay...but I thought love would be more. That it would overwhelm me."

"It will when it happens."

"That's what you feel for Quinn? You just can't tell her?" Caden nodded.

"What about Mary?"

"I thought that was love, but my feelings for Quinn are so much stronger. I was young with Mary, and I probably mistook lust for love."

Cathleen looked away. "I don't want to make a mistake…"

"Like I did?"

"I'm not trying to be mean, but it's in the back of my mind."

Caden shrugged. "Understandable. So did you end it?"

"No. In the summer, a new woman joined the crew. Her name is Regina, but she likes to be called Reggie." Cathleen took a shuddering breath.

Oh man. While Cath was trying to figure out what she felt for Larken, he fell for this new woman and jilted her. "Cath…" Caden reached his hand out to touch her shoulder.

"I know what you're thinking. And you're wrong. Reggie and I became close friends. She was new to town and didn't know many people. We did all kinds of things together, went to plays, concerts, and tried new restaurants. Sometimes on Friday night, we'd decompress with a movie night. There were nights I slept at her place. I was still spending time with Lark, just not as much." She got up to use the bathroom.

Caden wondered where she was leading. *She said there was nothing holding her in North Carolina, so obviously, Lark is out of the picture. She's about to make a big revelation.*

Cath walked out to his kitchen and opened the fridge. "Don't you have any water in here?"

"Use the tap, glasses are on the right."

"Of course they are." She laughed. "Just like at home." She returned to the couch and took a deep breath before starting to talk. "A couple of months ago, Larken accused me of being in love with Reggie." Cathleen looked at Caden, her eyes serious. "We had a terrible fight about it. I never saw Mom and Dad fight like we did that night. He was screaming, I was screaming, we hurled terrible insults." She raised the glass of water to her mouth. "Cade, he was accusing me of being gay."

"There's nothing wrong with lesbians Cath."

"I know that. But at the moment, it felt terrible. The next day, he called and asked me to meet him. We both apologized for the things we said, but Lark said he couldn't wait any longer for me to fall in love with him."

"I'm sorry."

"One of us needed to make that move. I gave you a hard time earlier about how long you'd known Quinn, but really, after a year, I was no closer to loving Lark than I was when I met him. I know it doesn't take that long. It stung for a few days, but I was okay. He moved to a different rowing group, so we didn't have to run into each other."

"Only a few days?"

"My lack of distress is proof I wasn't in love with him. I still had my friends, my life. I was fine." Cathleen paused, looking around the room and avoiding her brother's eyes. Finally, she placed her glass on the coffee table and met Caden's eyes.

"With Larken out of the picture, I had more time to spend with Reggie. Lark was gone, but his words played over and over and over and I wondered. Was what I felt for her more than just friendship? I wrestled hard with that. I mean, Brady's aren't gay..."

Caden interrupted her. "Stop that! There are no rules to being a Brady."

Cathleen rolled her eyes at him. "I remember plenty of rules growing up."

"There were. But we're all adults now and we're each our own person. No one is going to think less of you." This was a heavier conversation than he'd ever had with Cathleen and wasn't where he had expected the evening to go. *She needs a sounding board and I'm glad I'm here for her.* "What happened Cath? There's no judgement here."

"Reggie had never told me she was gay, but she also never expressed any interest in men. About a month ago, we were watching a movie..." Cathleen took a deep breath and looked away. "I kissed her."

Caden watched as Cathleen's face settled into a mixture of joy and despair. He moved to the couch and put his arm over her shoulder, giving her time to collect herself.

As she leaned against him, Cathleen said softly, "It was like I'd never kissed anyone in my entire life. It stirred desires I didn't know existed."

My sister is gay. Caden took a deep breath. *And it's okay.*

"When the kiss ended, Reggie pushed me away. She said at best I was bi and at worst I was only experimenting. That she came out at fourteen and she had no interest in shepherding me through that process. She was only interested in individuals who were secure in their sexuality, and I obviously wasn't." Tears had leaked down Cathleen's cheeks as she was talking. "It was brutal Cade. I had all this yearning coursing through my body, and she wanted nothing to do with me. This stung for more than a few days. It still stings. I lost my best friend." Her voice broke. "And on top of that, I don't know who I am anymore."

Caden held her as she wept. When she quieted, he pulled away so he could see her face. "I'm so sorry none of us were there to support you. I know how important that is. Did you have anyone?"

Cathleen shook her head. "No one knows what happened. You're the first one I've told." She wiped her hand across her face. "I'd already started looking for jobs and when the job in New Hampshire came up, I jumped on it. I can't stay in North Carolina any longer."

Chapter Seven

The Ski Trip

Caden

IT WAS SNOWING THE next weekend when Caden left Boston, and the farther north he drove, the heavier the snow came down. He silently thanked Quinn for his snow tires.

As he drove, he thought about how relieved he was to have his history with Mary out in the open at last, as well as how his grandfather had died and made Caden a very wealthy man. He'd been comparing his experience with Quinn to the beginning of his relationship with Mary, and even without the difference in maturity levels, he now knew there was no comparison. His love for Quinn was all-encompassing, and he wanted to spend the rest of his life with her.

I didn't think I'd ever feel this way again. And it still scares me.

Caden parked at Quinn's town house, and she ran out to his car. He gently brushed away the snowflakes in her hair. "Don't we need to take your skis?" She was wearing the cashmere scarf he gave her for Christmas, and he tugged gently on it to bring her lips to his before she could respond.

"I leave all my ski stuff at my parents' condo." She grinned at him. "Aren't you glad you have snow tires?"

Caden laughed, shaking his head. "You like winning arguments just a little too much."

After they resumed the drive, Quinn asked, "How's Ned? When we talked last night, you said he might get out of the ICU today."

"He did. I checked in on him before I left the hospital. He'll probably stay over the weekend at least. A social worker is trying to find space for him in a shelter."

"Will he be okay with that?"

"I think so. I've been going to that encampment for over a year and even as sick as Ned was, he looks better now than I've ever seen him. A warm place to sleep and three good meals every day makes a big difference." Caden reached for her hand. "I wish there was a place for every one of them."

Caden picked his way carefully along the snow-covered interstate, slowing when Quinn told him they were approaching notoriously slippery spots. "I've never been this far north."

They finally made it to the hotel around nine. Quinn texted with her mom to let her know they wouldn't see her until morning.

As soon as they reached the hotel room, they went after each other hungrily. "God, I've missed you," Caden groaned.

They tore each other's clothes off and fell onto the bed. After a few breathless minutes, Caden jumped up and rummaged through his bag, looking for the box of condoms he had thrown in while packing. "I can't wait until we don't have to bother with this."

She nodded. "No exploring tonight. I want you, and I want you now!"

After they climaxed and were lying side by side, Caden looked at the ceiling. "Did you tell your parents about Mary? Or my grandfather and the trust fund?" This had been on his mind all week. He knew it was stupid, but they were details about his life that embarrassed him in different ways.

Quinn climbed out of bed and went to the closet, taking out two robes. "Let's sit in the living room and enjoy the fireplace."

Caden opened the bottle of wine they had brought and poured two glasses. He handed one to Quinn, and they snuggled in front of the warm fire.

"I didn't tell my parents about any of that. It's not something they need to know. There was a time when my mother's only desire was for me to date someone with a job, a car, and a driver's license." Quinn smiled ruefully. "You obviously meet her criteria."

"That's a low bar to hit, Quinn. Did you really go out with guys who didn't have all of that?"

"Sadly, I did. I treated Sam badly after I left for college, and our breakup tanked my self-esteem. I felt like I didn't deserve someone with more to offer. In Boston, he and I talked about how we broke up, and I finally realized it wasn't all on me. I think getting there, finding that closure, made me ready for you."

He kissed her gently. "You're telling me I have something to be grateful to Sam for, huh?"

"Yeah, I guess I am." She nodded, looking thoughtful. "It took me a long time to remember the good parts of him and our relationship."

"Can I ask how you mistreated him?" Caden didn't want to think it, but he wondered if she had cheated on Sam.

Quinn took a deep breath and held it for several seconds before exhaling. Her hand at her mouth, she tapped her teeth.

Caden recognized this as a sign she was uncomfortable. Taking her hand in his, he said, "You don't have to tell me."

"No, it's okay. I told you I was a geek in high school. I landed in that niche early on, and none of the guys other than Sam paid any attention to me. When I got to college, I wasn't in that niche. The college guys didn't know me as a geek, and they talked to me, flirted with me. I was curious. Sam was the only man I'd ever been with, and I wondered what other guys would be like." She sighed again. "I didn't know what to do. So, I took the easy way out. I started ignoring Sam. I didn't answer his calls. If he texted, I waited a long time before responding, or I didn't respond at all."

Her hand went back to her mouth, and she tapped her lips again.

Caden leaned in to kiss her, taking her hand in his. "You're okay."

She nodded. "We finally talked and agreed to take a break for a few weeks. When we did... there was a guy who paid a lot of attention to me. I wasn't a drinker, meaning campus parties weren't much fun. He'd do other things with me." She shook her head. "He told me I was saving him from a hangover. We went to a movie one night, then back to my room to watch another movie in the same series."

She gave half a half-hearted shrug. "You can imagine how that ended. I quickly figured out sex was all he wanted. He treated me nothing like Sam had, and I realized I made a mistake. I contacted Sam, and I lied when he asked if I had been with anyone else."

Caden found that didn't hit like he'd feared. She'd been so young then.

Quinn went on. "But I told a friend, and it traveled back to him. I came home on break, thinking we were going to have a wonderful reunion, and instead, we had a terrible argument. When I reached out by text to apologize and beg him to forgive me, Sam spelled out all my failings in great detail. How I was an untrustworthy liar, had thrown away our love, didn't deserve to be treated well, and now he wanted nothing to do with me. It left me feeling worthless." She seemed to shrink into herself. "From then on, I picked guys who were as different from Sam as possible. I didn't think I deserved a good guy or even knew what a good guy was."

Caden hugged her. "You didn't deserve that. You were what, eighteen?"

"Well, nineteen. In Boston, he told me that when we agreed to take a break, the girl he'd been running into at a bar started stroking his ego, and it ramped up into a relationship. His tirade toward *me* had come from *her*. She told him what to text me. What he said didn't reflect his feelings, and it's haunted him all these years."

She took a swallow of her wine. "I'd started therapy when I arrived at Dartmouth. Sam telling me the truth, opened the final door for me. It made me realize I deserve to be treated well, and I have something to bring to a relationship. And then you came along." She smiled at him.

Caden nodded. "Knowing he was already with someone else when he treated you that way—it didn't make you angry?"

"Just as my friend told him what I'd done, our mutual friends let me know he was seeing someone. I spent ten years being angry at him. Somehow, hearing the truth let me forgive him. And forgive myself. Getting rid of that anger has been good for me."

Caden hugged her, knowing he was not at that point with Mary and didn't know if he ever would be.

Saturday morning dawned with a cold, blue January sky. Their room was on the west side of the hotel, and Caden was surprised when Quinn bounded out of bed and pulled on a robe as soon as she opened her eyes. "What's got you leaving my side?"

He watched her push back the drapes. "I can't wait to show you one of my favorite views in the entire world!" She tossed the other robe to him.

Caden put it on and joined Quinn at the window, which looked out at the break in the mountains known as Willoughby Gap. "Whoa, that's very cool." The sky was brilliant blue, and snow blanketed the mountain peaks.

"It takes my breath away every time. Willoughby Lake is one of my favorite places. We won't go there this weekend, but we must go up there in the summer. There's great hiking, and the lake water is crystal clear."

They went to her parents' condo, where Quinn introduced him in person. "Mom, Dad, again, this is Caden. Caden, my parents, Henry and Melanie Michaels."

Caden shook their hands. "It's nice to meet you in person."

Quinn's dad raised a finger. "Remember, it's Hank and Mel, please. If you call us mister and missus, we feel like we're back in school. And we don't want to go back there, do we, honey?"

Mel nodded and urged them to sit down for breakfast. Quinn had told Caden Hank had been a middle school principal and Mel was a teacher. He asked how long ago they had retired.

"Four years ago, as soon as I was eligible," Mel said. "Hank does consulting, but we're glad to be out of the day-to-day grind."

"Quinn said you spend the winter in Florida. My parents just bought a house in Fort Myers so they can escape the winter."

"We're in Venice, a bit north of Fort Myers. There's nothing like sitting on the beach and knowing that it's below zero back here." Mel smiled at Quinn. "Only because Quinn asked us would we stay longer than two weeks up here in the frozen tundra."

Quinn's father chimed in. "I miss skiing, but it's nice not having to deal with all the other aspects of winter."

"How much have you skied on this trip, Dad?"

Hank replied with a smile. "Every day."

"Mom, are you going to ski with us?" Quinn asked. She winked at Caden, and he was sure she already knew how her mother was going to answer.

"No, I'm going to stay warm in the condo this morning, and I have a lunch date with a couple of my old colleagues. I'll see you at the hotel restaurant tonight."

After breakfast, Quinn took Caden to the base lodge for lift tickets and rental gear. While they were waiting for Caden to be fitted with skis, he said, "My God, you didn't tell me your dad was so big! I don't run into a lot of men who are taller than I am. And you look like your mother."

"Dad's size came in handy when he was a principal. He's very intimidating. He'll probably tell you the kids caused him to lose his hair. I wish I had a little of his height instead of being short like my mother." She gave him a quick kiss. "I think they liked you."

Quinn watched Caden glide over the flat area outside the base lodge and, after a few minutes, said, "Let's try the J-Bar. I want to see how you do on the hill." When they reached the bottom, she said, "I knew you'd be good at this. Try to relax and remember to bend your knees. I think you can handle the chairlift."

At the top, they skied away from the lift and turned to face down the mountain. The view over the valley took Caden's breath away, and he stumbled, then slid on his butt for several feet.

Quinn skied over to him. "Are you okay?" She watched as he struggled to get up. "Do you want some help?"

"Nope, nope. Give me a minute, I'll figure it out." He finally placed his skis parallel to each other, and stood up. "Everything's fine except my ego."

Quinn shook her head. "Everyone falls. Are you ready to tackle the hill?"

Caden nodded, and Quinn led him down the mountain. They went up the lift several more times, with Hank joining them on the last one. At the bottom, Quinn said, "Do you mind if I do a few runs with my dad? You could find us a table in the lodge." She skied closer so she could kiss him. "You did really well, much better than I did on skates."

Caden went inside while Quinn did some more advanced trails with her father. A wall of windows allowed him to see Quinn skiing. *She's so fast and so graceful, but she was so patient with me.* The bubble of emotion he'd felt so often welled up in his chest again. *I love her.*

Chapter Eight
Lunch With Sam

Caden

PEOPLE STARTED COMING IN for lunch, and a man with a young girl caught his eye. After a minute, he realized it was Sam. The girl had to be his daughter. Caden's heart raced, and he took several deep breaths to get himself under control. It had not crossed his mind they were in Sam's old stomping grounds, and might run into him.

Caden watched them intently as they stood in line. Sam focused totally on his daughter, talking and laughing with her as they moved toward the counter. After they ordered, they walked into the dining area, searching unsuccessfully for an open table.

Caden took a deep breath and thought, *God, I'm probably going to regret this,* before he called, "Sam! Hey, Sam." As Sam turned to the sound of his voice, Caden waved, and Sam approached with a confused smile on his face. "Caden Brady. We met in Boston. You're welcome to sit here."

Sam pulled out a chair for the girl, then joined her at the table. He said, "I was not expecting to run into you here."

"Quinn and I are here visiting her parents. She and her dad are on the slopes. They should come in for lunch soon." Caden watched Sam carefully. He wanted to be sure Sam understood he and Quinn were together—and he tried not to think about Sam sleeping with Quinn in Boston.

"This is my daughter, Piper," Sam said. "She had her first lesson this morning. Piper, this is Dr. Brady."

Caden offered his hand to the girl. "I'm pleased to meet you, Piper. Did your lesson go well?"

She shook his hand in a very adult way. "Yes, I only fell twice. D-Daddy said that was great for my first t-time. After lunch, we're going to ski t-together. Do you ski?"

Caden grinned, charmed. "I'm a beginner, just like you. I didn't take a lesson, though, because my girlfriend thought she could teach me." He was happy to refer to Quinn as his girlfriend.

Just then, Quinn and Hank entered the lodge, and Caden raised his arm, so they'd see him. Caden watched as Quinn realized who was sitting at the table. Her eyes opened wide in surprise, and her father's did the same.

"Sam?" she said. "This is a surprise."

"Sam Carpenter," Hank said. "It's been a long time."

Sam stood to shake Hank's hand. "All the tables were full, and Dr. Brady invited us to share his. This is my daughter, Piper. Piper, this is Quinn Michaels and her dad, Mr. Michaels. They are old friends of mine."

Piper stood and offered her hand for them to shake, as Caden had done with her.

Caden could see Sam being at the table rattled Quinn. He smiled at her reassuringly and suggested they go to the counter to order. "Your dad and Sam can catch up."

As they walked away from the table, she hissed, "What the hell! That was the last thing I expected to see when I walked into the lodge. How did Sam and his daughter end up sitting with you?"

"I recognized him, and all the tables were full. It seemed like the right thing to do. And I enjoyed being able to tell him I was here with you and to refer to you as my girlfriend. His daughter's cute."

She took a breath and let it out. "Are you okay?"

He knew what she was asking. "More or less. My heart started pounding when I saw him, but it calmed down. Did you tell your parents you saw him in Boston? And tried to rekindle things?"

"No, I was too busy talking about you." She smiled. "And there was no reason to. He's the past, remember?"

He gave her a brief hug while they waited to order. By the time they returned to the table, Sam had filled Hank in on the highlights of his encounter with Quinn in Boston. The conversation was congenial while they ate, and Caden rested his hand on Quinn's leg the entire time.

As they cleared the table, Piper asked, "Do you want to see me ski?"

Caden responded for all of them. "We'd love to watch you ski."

Sam handed Hank his phone, asking if he'd take a video of them.

As they walked to the bunny hill, Caden put his arm over Quinn's shoulder. The three of them watched Sam and Piper ride up the magic carpet, and Caden asked, "Why didn't I get to do that?"

Quinn smirked at him. "I knew you could handle a harder lift."

When they reached the bottom of the slope, Piper and Sam skied over to let Sam retrieve his phone, and Piper gave each of them a quick hug.

Sam looked at Caden, nodding. "Thanks for giving us a place to sit. It was nice to see all of you. Enjoy your visit."

While Quinn talked with her father about the mountain, Caden thought about the encounter with Sam. *I built him into a mythic creature Quinn couldn't resist, and after watching her reaction, I know that's not true. I didn't see anything more than friendship between them. Sam's dedicated to his daughter. And what a sweet little girl she is—too bad about the stutter.*

Sam had told Caden how fast and fearless Quinn had been on the high school team, and her father had described an epic fall she had taken her senior year. *I like how they gave me a picture of what Quinn was like back then. And I like that the deep breathing suggested in therapy helped me through my initial reaction to seeing Sam.*

I think I'm finally getting over this.

Quinn

Quinn told her father she was going to give Caden a tour and they would meet at the restaurant for dinner. As they walked to his car, Caden handed her his keys.

"You're letting me drive?"

"You know where you're going, and I want to look around. Did it kill you to ski so slowly with me? You were very patient."

"Not at all. I taught lessons one day a week, for little kids, when I was in high school. Dad was on the ski patrol." She made a left turn, then slowed and pointed at a cream-colored house.

"That's the house I grew up in." After giving him a minute to study it, she drove to a short street lined with shops. "This is downtown. Don't blink, you'll miss it."

They passed a football field and Quinn said, "This was my high school. Those buildings down there." She pointed back to where they had come from. "And these up here." They were climbing a hill with a stately building on the right.

"It's a pretty campus, even covered with snow."

"It is," Quinn agreed as she continued driving up the hill. "This is the state college. It's one of four. I took a couple of dual enrollment classes my senior year in high school, so I had some college credits when I graduated."

"Smarty pants. Can you park for a minute?" he asked.

"Who are you calling smarty? I didn't get a scholarship to Boston University." she turned into a parking spot in the college lot. "Why do you want to stop?"

Caden unbuckled his seatbelt and leaned over to kiss her. "To do this. You can't imagine how much it turned me on to let Sam know you're my girlfriend." They kissed for several minutes, and he unzipped her coat, sliding his hands under her sweater.

She groaned. "There's a perfectly good hotel room waiting for us on the mountain. We are not having sex in this car."

Reluctantly, he sat back in his seat and buckled the seatbelt. "Then you better get driving." He put his hand on her leg and let it wander as she drove back to the mountain.

As soon as they closed the hotel-room door, he pushed her against it and lowered his mouth to hers. They kissed roughly as he unzipped her jacket and jerked it off. Her sweater came off next, allowing him to take her nipple in his mouth as his hands unzipped her pants and shoved them to the floor.

"God, between claiming you as my girlfriend and watching you on skis, I want you more than I ever have." He lifted her up and carried her to the bed. She watched, her heart pounding and her clit throbbing, as he ripped his clothes off.

Naked, he unsnapped her bra and reached for her thong before pulling it down and driving two fingers into her. She pushed against them and pulled his head to her breasts. As soon as his tongue flicked her nipple, she came with a moan. He continued to stroke her as wave after wave pulsed through her body.

As her release subsided, her hand found his cock and began stroking it from balls to tip. Groaning, his hips thrust toward her. She abruptly changed her position and took him in her mouth. As she sucked and fondled him, he grew even harder. She paused for a moment, and he pushed toward her, letting her know he wanted her to continue. She felt his climax coming and took as much of him as possible into her mouth. His orgasm came with a shout, and she swallowed, then continued to suck him until his trembling stopped.

Quinn crawled up his body and took his face in her hands. "It was such a turn-on seeing you in the lodge, being so kind."

They took a brief nap entwined in each other's arms, and when they woke up, Caden was hard again, and Quinn took him inside her. Afterward, they showered and dressed for dinner. Quinn checked her phone and found a message from Sam.

She showed it to Caden, and he admitted it had gone better than he expected. "What are we doing tomorrow?"

"We'll visit my parents before we leave. Why? Is there something you want to do?"

"Can we go to the top of the mountain?"

"Do you want to ski from the top?" Her tone was hesitant.

"God no. But I'd like to see the view from up there. I know you like it. Do you have to ski to ride the chairlift?"

"No. Do you want to get off at the top or just ride right back down? There's not much up there. Just a fire tower." She grinned at him. "I can guarantee you won't want to climb it."

Caden smiled back. "No, probably not. I would like to get off, though. Can we just walk around a bit? Watch the crazy people who fling themselves down the mountain on narrow slats?"

"Sounds fun. Let's go first thing in the morning, when it's quiet. Then we can stop at the condo."

Caden nodded in agreement.

Caden

As they approached the lift early on Sunday morning, the attendant, an older man, opened his arms. "Quinn Michaels. Where have you been all winter?"

Quinn walked into his arms for a brief hug. "Winter's just starting. I've been busy. Fred, this is my boyfriend, Caden Brady. Cade, this is Fred, the best liftie on the mountain."

"Where's your skis girl? This is the best snow we've had in years."

The chairs came up behind them and as they were carried away, Quinn called, "We skied yesterday. It's good to see you, Fred."

Caden grasped her hand as they soared further and further from the ground. *Her boyfriend. God, I love hearing that.* "Do you know everyone on the mountain? I'm amazed at how many people greeted you by name."

"I told you," Quinn snickered. "Small town life is not anonymous. And many people, once they work on the mountain, just keep coming back every winter. I try to ski here a couple of times a year, so they remember me."

The air was perfectly still and silent as they glided up the mountain. Quinn squeezed his hand. "I love it when there's no sound." Near the top, the silence was shattered by two snowboarders who were whooping and hollering as they traversed the slopes. The lift reached the summit, they disembarked, and looked out over the valley before Quinn led him away. "Let's walk up to the fire tower."

"I enjoy hearing you call me your boyfriend." Caden pulled her close.

"I enjoy saying it." She gestured at their surroundings. "What do you think?"

"It's stunning." The fire tower came into view and Caden swore. "Damn, people climb that. It looks ready to fall over."

"It's about eighty years old. I did a research paper on fire towers when I was in high school."

"Have you climbed it?"

"Yup."

Caden shuddered as they walked toward the tower. He leaned against it and embraced Quinn. "I feel like we're on top of the world." He held her for a minute, drinking in the silence, then moved her away so he could see her face. "I love you. I didn't want to say it in the throes of passion, because it's so much more than just the physical connection we have. You're amazing and I'm..." He took a deep breath. "I'm so happy you're in my life. I love you." He lowered his lips to hers in a gentle kiss. "You're going to tire of hearing me say it."

"Never." Quinn caressed his cheek. "You planned this? Coming to the top of the mountain even though it makes you uncomfortable. That's... I don't even know. You do the most romantic things. I'm so glad we found each other. I love you too,"

Quinn and Caden were nearly ready to leave her parents' condo when she and her mother decided to visit a nearby bakery. As Hank and Caden watched a football game, Hank asked, "Did Quinn tell you about her history with Sam?"

"Yes, she told me early on."

"The end of that relationship left her hurting. Truthfully, it hurt us too. We'd taken him in like a son and he just disappeared." Hank threw up his hands. "But that's neither here nor there. You have nothing to worry about from him. I've never seen her as happy as she is with you."

Caden's heart warmed at Hank's words. "It's nice to hear you say that. She's the best thing that's happened to me in a long time."

Chapter Nine

Their Second Fight

Quinn

"WHAT A PASS!" QUINN threw her arms around Caden, cheering, after the Patriots' quarterback drilled a perfect pass into the end zone to tie the game with seconds left on the clock. Brooke was sitting with them since Danny was with the media team, and she pounded on Caden's back in excitement too.

They returned their attention to the field, holding their breath, waiting to see if the kicker would be successful in the extra-point attempt. As the football sailed through the goalposts, the stadium erupted in pandemonium, and all three of them hugged.

The two couples had met for dinner midweek at a restaurant halfway between Hanover and Boston, and Brooke was much warmer than she had been at the hockey game. Caden took care to make sure Quinn didn't feel left out as the three friends talked about shared experiences and people Quinn had not yet met.

Brooke insisted on exchanging phone numbers with Quinn, who had been surprised and pleased the next day when Brooke's first text arrived. The women had similar interests, and Quinn was starting to think they might become friends. She suspected Caden may have had something to do with Brooke's change in attitude. She questioned him when she arrived at his home on Friday night, and he admitted telling Brooke that he could take care of himself and to give Quinn a chance.

Danny texted Brooke when he was ready to go, and they made their way down to the field. Caden clapped him on the shoulder. "Great game, man! Thanks for the tickets!"

Danny put his arm around Brooke. "Let's go get some dinner and celebrate."

They chattered all the way back to Boston, reviewing every play. As they approached the city, Danny asked Caden, "What's it going to be? O'Malley's or the Tavern?"

"O'Malley's. Then Quinn and I can walk home. Plus, we can shoot some darts after we eat."

Caden and Danny hung out there often enough that they were well-known, and as the four of them walked through the bar, several people stopped Danny to congratulate him on the team's win.

Finally at their table, Quinn looked at Danny and quipped, "Celebrity is such a pain." They all laughed and ordered drinks to celebrate.

Caden raised his glass. "On to the Superbowl!"

As they touched their glasses, Danny reminded them, "We need to win one more game before that."

They each ordered fish and chips, and Caden and Danny finished their meals with a shot of Irish whiskey. Danny eyed the dartboard. "Are we going girls against boys?"

Brooke looked at Quinn, and she shrugged.

While Danny was preparing to launch a dart, Quinn's watch buzzed with a text from Ashley, and although she tried not to be on her phone in social situations, this was a question needing an answer. Taking out her phone, she typed a quick response, then put it back in her pocket.

She was the next one up and her concentration was on the dartboard when Caden asked, "Who was that?"

Quinn lined up the dart and threw a perfect bullseye.

As she high-fived Brooke, Caden asked again, "Who was that?" Quinn looked at him quizzically, and he motioned toward her pocket. "On the phone."

"Oh, it was Ashley. Someone had an HR question, and she thought I'd know the answer."

They played several more games before they left to walk to Caden's.

As soon as they walked in the door, Quinn embraced him and sought his lips. She kissed him deeply, thrusting her tongue into his open mouth. After a few moments, she pulled back. "Today was outstanding! Thank you!"

He pushed her against the wall and snaked his hand under her sweater. His head ducked to reach her breast with his mouth, but she pushed him away. "I need to pee. Hold that thought. I'll be right back."

He groaned. "You're killing me. Don't take too long."

She took off her jacket and put her phone on the shelf before heading to the bathroom. She returned to find Caden holding her phone.

Her eyes narrowed. "What are you doing?"

"I was, um, looking for a sexy playlist."

She cocked her head. The phone was in plain sight, and the screen wasn't on playlists. He put it down, shame on his face, and she said, incredulously, "Were you checking up on me? Looking at my text messages?"

He nodded sheepishly.

"Why? What did you think you'd find?"

He sighed. "You hesitated when I asked who texted you at the pub. I wondered if it really was Ashley."

Her eyes widened. "I was getting ready to throw a *dart!* Who did you think it was?"

Caden rubbed his jaw but did not answer.

"You thought it was Sam, didn't you?"

He nodded. "I'm sorry." His arms went toward her, but she stepped back out of his reach. Her heart was pounding, and she remembered something from the hotel the week before.

"This isn't the first time, either. You looked at my phone when I was in the shower last Sunday."

He didn't deny it.

Unbelievable. "Have I given you any reason to think I'm talking to Sam? I've let you know anytime I hear from him." She was trying to control her voice, but it was shaking with agitation.

"I just... you hesitated tonight... I thought you were hiding something." He reached for her again, and she waved him off, shaking her head.

"What more can I do?"

"Babe, I'm sorry. I know..."

"Don't babe me. I'm going home. I can't stay here." Quinn walked into the bathroom, gathered her toiletries, and dumped them into her suitcase, which was open on the bed in the guest room. She grabbed her clothes and tossed them in before slamming the suitcase shut.

Caden was waiting for her when she emerged. "You can't drive home tonight. It's late, and you've been drinking."

"I know what time it is, and I had wine with dinner. That was hours ago. I'm fine to drive." She shrugged on her jacket, pushing his hands away as he tried to help her. She opened the door to go down the stairs. He followed her, trying to grab the suitcase. "Go away. I don't need your help."

"I'm not letting you walk to the parking garage alone in the middle of the night. Please, Quinn, stop. We can talk about it."

"We can talk when you stop acting like a jealous fifteen-year-old with his first girlfriend!" She strode purposefully to the garage, put the suitcase in the back seat, and climbed into the driver's seat. By then, tears were leaking from her eyes as she turned the key in the ignition.

Caden had his hand on the roof of the car. She rolled down the window and angrily brushed the tears away. "The night we lay under the Christmas tree, you asked me if I got off on being mistreated because you couldn't do that. Well, I don't get off on jealousy either. Please, let me go. I can't be with you right now."

He slowly removed his hand from the car and moved out of the way. "Let me know when you get home, please."

She nodded and drove out of the garage. Two hours later, she sent him a text.

> I'm home.

Quinn sent the text to Caden, letting him know she'd gotten home safely, before crawling into bed. She'd been shaking throughout the drive home, tears filling her eyes nearly the entire time. Her thoughts kept going back to her teen years and dating Sam. He had become obsessed with checking her phone, always wanting to know who she was texting. It had been a huge stumbling block between them even before she left for college.

She couldn't do that again. Couldn't be with someone who was constantly checking on her. Caden told her about his trust issues, and she understood them. It was why she told him whenever Sam sent a text. There hadn't been very many. Thankfully, Sam was respecting her boundaries.

Was leaving the right move? Should I have stayed and talked it out?

No. *I'm so angry. I couldn't talk to him tonight. And I couldn't be in his home.*

She turned over, her eyes aching.

Oh God, did I do the same thing Mary did by leaving? What must he be thinking—feeling?

No, it's not the same. I did what he asked and let him know when I got home. He knows where I am.

I love him. How the hell are we going to get past this? She stopped fighting the tears that had been threatening since she left Boston and sobbed until sleep overtook her.

In the morning, Quinn threw her bathing suit and a towel into her bag and drove to the pool. She changed quickly with all the times she'd sent bathing suit pictures to Caden flitting through her mind. Once she jumped into the pool, she started viciously drawing her arms through the water, concentrating on breathing and form, swimming as fast as she could. Her anger hammered into every stroke.

After several laps, Quinn slowed her pace and let her mind wander. She couldn't imagine her life without Caden, but couldn't spend the rest of her life with someone who was going to question every text or call. Tears threatened again as she floated on her back to cool down.

She climbed out of the pool and came face-to-face with Izzy, who immediately asked, "What are you doing here, and why are you tearing through the water like you're training to swim the English Channel?"

Quinn gazed at her, pondering how to respond. She blinked back tears. "Don't let me hold you up. Go ahead and get in the water."

"Quinn, I already swam. I'd just gotten out when you blew by me, so I waited for you. I thought you were in Boston this weekend, at that football game. What's going on?"

Quinn's face crumpled, and she angrily wiped at the tears coursing down her cheeks. She started to speak, stopped, and brought her hand to her mouth as she shook her head.

"What's wrong?" Izzy looked alarmed. When Quinn couldn't answer, Izzy said, "Come to brunch with me. Please."

Quinn nodded. As she stood in the shower, she let the tears flow while the water cascaded over her. *This is ridiculous! I have to get myself under control!*

Izzy was dressed and waiting when Quinn finally stepped out of the shower. "Let's go to Java Junction. I know you like it there."

Quinn nodded. "I'm sorry," she said. "I'll have myself together by the time we get there."

Izzy arrived at the restaurant first, and there were two cups of coffee on the table when Quinn slid into her seat. "If you want alcohol, you'll have to order it." Izzy smiled. "Three more months until I turn twenty-one."

Quinn took a long swallow, then drew a deep breath. "Thanks. This is fine."

"You were the last person I expected to see at the rec center," Izzy said. "I thought when you made the trip to see your bae you stayed all weekend."

"I caught him looking at my text messages last night." Quinn said, studying the table. "I guess... I'm embarrassed to tell you that. I drove home in the middle of the night."

"Embarrassed?" Izzy's voice rose an octave. "He's the one who should be embarrassed! That's a huge red flag."

"It's complicated." Quinn had no intention of sharing Caden's history with Izzy. *But I must give her some explanation.* "He has some trust issues."

Izzy scoffed. "Trust issues? Come on."

"I can't go into it all, but there's a reason for it. Trust me." Quinn managed a small, sad laugh.

"Because of something you did?" Izzy shook her head. "I'll never believe that. I can tell you're totally gone for him. You'd never do anything to make him salty."

Izzy's quick defense made Quinn feel a little better. She appreciated her young friend's righteous indignation on her behalf. "Nothing I did. Something from a prior relationship."

"And are you going to put up with that?" Izzy's voice still rang with displeasure.

"I want to help him overcome it. Last night, I was too angry to do that, so I came home." *And I'm still not sure it was the right move.*

After they ordered food, Quinn took a deep breath and eyed Izzy. "Aren't you back early? Classes don't start until mid-January, right?"

"Are you changing the subject?"

"Maybe." Quinn sighed. "I need to get out of my head, so tell me what's going on with you."

"It was boring at home." Izzy played with a lock of her hair. "And you know that guy I mentioned talking to before the break?"

"Ethan?" Quinn smiled.

"Yeah. He came back to town right after New Year's... and he's the only one at his apartment..."

"Izzy! You bad girl! You came back for a guy."

"We're just hanging out!"

"Uh-huh, sure you are." Quinn laughed at the blush coloring Izzy's cheeks.

They spent an hour at the restaurant, and when they stood to leave, Quinn put her arms around Izzy. "Thanks for this. I would have just gone home and moped about what happened." She rolled her eyes at herself. "Not to say I won't do that now, but you gave me a brief respite."

Izzy hugged her back. "Don't let him make you feel bad. This is not your fault."

At home, Quinn went through the motions of getting ready for the week and tried to figure out what more she could do to let Caden know he could trust her. Before the weekend, she had made plans to meet Ashley at the Sidecar that evening, not knowing how much she would need that. Talking to Izzy had been a great boost, but as with most twenty-year-olds, everything was black or white with her. Quinn hoped Ashley would see the shades of gray and better understand Quinn's turmoil.

Ashley arrived at the restaurant first, and there were two margaritas on the table when Quinn slid into her seat. She took a long swallow, then drew in a deep breath as she felt the alcohol warm her. "Thanks. This is exactly what I needed."

"You saw a great game! Tell me all about it."

"It was an amazing game. We had a great time. But then…" Quinn shook her head and described finding Caden looking at her phone. When she was done, she was on the verge of tears again. "I couldn't stay. I've told you how Sam did that kind of thing."

Ashley put a hand on Quinn's. "Damn, my text started it all. I'm sorry."

"No, no, don't do that. It's an issue, and if it hadn't come up last night, something else would have sparked it. I mean, it wasn't the first time."

Ashley nodded. "Have you heard from him?"

"He asked me to text when I was home. I did that, but nothing else. He didn't respond to my text."

"You're not through with him." Ashley's expression was somber. "You wouldn't be this torn up if you were."

"Oh, no, I'm not." Quinn sighed. "I love him with all my heart, but I don't know what more I can do to make him know I can be trusted."

They stayed at the restaurant for a couple of hours, with Ashley listening as Quinn replayed every moment of the day before. When they stood to leave, Ashley gave Quinn a hug.

Quinn leaned into her friend. "Thank you for listening to me. I'm sure this wasn't the conversation you expected, but I feel a little better now."

Quinn went to bed as soon as she got home, but sleep was beyond reach. As she tossed and turned, she remembered they were supposed to have dinner with Caden's parents that day.

Did he go without me? Would he have told them what had happened? God, what they'll think of me...

At ten thirty, her phone dinged, and her heart jumped as she picked it up.

Caden: How are you?

Quinn: Shitty. You?

Caden: Same.

Caden: I don't know what to say other than to tell you again how sorry I am.

Caden: I couldn't go the whole day without reaching out.

Quinn: I don't know what to say either.

Caden: I love you, Quinn Michaels, and we will figure this out.

She let the conversation end there, but it haunted her dreams all night.

Chapter Ten

Making Up

Caden

CADEN STRUGGLED THROUGH THE beginning of the week, not knowing what to think of Quinn's lack of response when he texted that he loved her on Sunday. He told his parents they couldn't come to dinner because Quinn was called back to Hanover to cover a shift. Lying didn't come easy, but he didn't want to admit what an idiot he had been, and he didn't want his family to think less of Quinn. She *was perfectly justified in leaving. I don't know why I was so stupid.*

On Tuesday night, Robbie came to work out, and Danny came with him. They made their way to the gym and rotated through the equipment. Robbie and Danny bantered about the Patriots' chances in the next game, but Caden stayed quiet.

As he was putting on boxing gloves to work on the punching bag, he saw Robbie catch Danny's eye and mouth, "What's up with him?" Danny just shrugged.

Caden went after the punching bag with a vengeance, trying to work out the frustration he'd been feeling since Quinn left on Saturday night. Robbie and Danny finished before him and watched as he battered the bag.

Finally, Danny stepped in. "Are you trying to kill that bag?" Caden didn't answer, so Danny grasped his shoulder. "Cade, what's going on?"

Caden stopped and backed away from the bag, not saying anything until he had removed the gloves. "I fucked up."

Danny looked surprised. "What? At the hospital?"

"No, with Quinn. On Saturday."

Caden had added a sauna to the gym as a Christmas present to himself, and he motioned for them to follow him into it.

Once they were settled, Danny spoke first. "What happened? Everything seemed fine when you left O'Malley's."

"It was until we got home. Remember how she got a text message and answered it?"

"Not really. Oh, wait a minute—you asked her who it was, and she said it was Ashley."

Caden described how she'd caught him looking at her phone, ending with "She was so pissed, she left."

"Left?" Robbie asked. "Where'd she go?"

"Back to New Hampshire."

"In the middle of the night?" Robbie asked incredulously.

"Yeah, she told me I was acting like a jealous fifteen-year-old with his first girlfriend." Caden put his head in his hands, looking at the floor.

Robbie kept going. "Have you talked to her since then?"

"We texted briefly. Well, I texted. She only gave me two curt responses."

"It's just a fight, Cade. You'll get by it," Danny said. "And then you get to have makeup sex." He grinned.

"I—I, Jesus, I don't know how to fight. Mary and I never fought."

Robbie looked at him in disbelief. "Dude. Everybody fights."

"We didn't. Maybe at the beginning, over petty stuff like what we were going to do on a date, but not once we were serious."

"Okay, I'm going to give you some tough love," Robbie said. "You didn't fight because you worked all the time. Between med school and your residency, you left her free to do whatever she wanted to. And we all know what she was doing. Why would she fight with you?"

Caden sighed. "That's harsh, man."

Danny chimed in. "But you know it's true."

"Yeah, I do. But I still don't know what to do about Quinn. What should I say to her?"

Robbie sighed. "You could plead temporary insanity. Or wait, had you been drinking?"

Caden nodded.

"Impaired judgment! There you go," Robbie snapped his fingers. "Two good pleas."

He and Danny laughed as Caden shook his head. "You guys are a riot." Still, they'd brought a glimmer of a smile to his face.

"Go see her." Danny clapped him on the shoulder. "You'll figure out what to say. And remember, makeup sex."

Robbie continued laughing. "And now you can take whatever you pay your therapist and split it between Danny and me."

Caden felt better after they left. *Just a fight. It was just a fight.* The conversation reminded him how delayed his emotional development was because of those nine years with Mary.

After thinking about it, Caden put some clothes in his backpack, planning to drive to Hanover as soon as his shift finished the next day. He hoped they could iron things out and Quinn would want him to spend the night with her.

As planned, Caden was in Quinn's parking lot when she drove in late Wednesday afternoon. She climbed out of her car and inclined her head toward him. He thought she was welcoming him, but he could see the tears in her eyes.

He walked toward her, and she said, voice even, "Fancy meeting you here."

Reaching for her tote bag, he was relieved she didn't resist him. "I realized I've never seen you on a Wednesday. I had to drive up."

They walked to her door, and when they were inside, Caden helped her with her coat. Her scrub top was royal blue. "That's the same top you had on when I saw you on the ward after Rory was born."

She nodded. "Showing off that memory again."

"I remember every moment we've had together." She sat in the chair, and he took the couch. "Can I start a fire?"

"Sure. Do you want something to drink? A beer?"

He walked to the fireplace. "Some water would be good."

She went to the kitchen, returning with a glass for each of them.

He took it. "My legal counsel advised me to plead impaired judgment because of the alcohol consumed. Or temporary insanity."

Quinn's lips quirked. "Robbie?"

"Yeah. Will either of those work?" He laughed a little to let her know he wasn't expecting a positive answer.

"Do you think they should?"

"I'd like to think I wouldn't have done it if I'd been stone-cold sober. But I don't know."

Quinn's expression crumpled. "I feel badly I left you like Mary did."

"No, don't say that. The circumstances are completely different. You told me you were leaving, and you let me know you were home. And I understand why you left." Max jumped into Caden's lap, and he started petting him.

"I was furious, and I don't like that feeling. I couldn't be there with you. But in retrospect, it was immature. I should have stayed and talked things out with you."

"Was I really acting like a jealous fifteen-year-old?"

Quinn took a deep breath. "The last year Sam and I were together, he was always checking my phone. He was older than fifteen, but that was all I could think of. I understand your trust issues, but I can't live like that, with every call or text being questioned."

"I've never thought of myself as a jealous person." Caden swallowed. "I accept the relationship you had with Sam. And that you've become friends. It's a trust thing. A little voice inside asked me if I believed it was Ashley, and then I had to know. I hate it!" He began to tremble. "You are open and honest with me. I know that." His voice was agitated. "I know it! Until I don't." He was burying his fingers in Max's fur like a lifeline, and he picked the cat up to nuzzle him the same way Quinn would.

"I know," she breathed. "It felt crappy to think we were fighting."

"For me too. I know I can survive without you, but my life is better knowing you're a part of it. Will you give me another chance?"

"Oh God, yes. I needed time to think about what I wanted to say and to figure out if there was something I could do to make it easier for you." She sighed. "Fighting is not my strong suit. I always thought a fight meant the end of the relationship, and I'd cave to whatever the guy wanted." She looked into his eyes. "I won't do that anymore."

"I don't want you to. We should be equal partners, working things out together." He let out a humorless breath. "I don't know how to fight either."

Quinn moved to sit beside him on the couch. "So, this is our second fight?"

"I guess."

"I don't like it any better than the first one. You talked to Danny and Rob?"

"Yeah, they want me to pay them what I pay my therapist. They're real comedians. What do we do now?"

"That's all I've thought about since Sunday. I promise you, I will continue to be honest and open about who I'm in contact with. My life is better with you in it, too." She leaned against him.

His heart thumped. "And I promise I will trust you. If I have doubts, I will let you know, and we can work through them together." He put his arms around her, content to feel her against him.

"Are you going back to Boston tonight?"

"That depends on you. I took tomorrow off."

She smiled. "Stay."

Chapter Eleven

Valentine's Day

Quinn

QUINN'S HEART SKIPPED A beat as she lit two red tapers and dimmed the light over the table. Chicken Piccata was ready on the stove and as soon as Caden arrived, she would cook angel hair pasta to go with it. They had not spent an entire weekend together since their trip to Vermont, and she was excited to spend two nights with him again.

Yeah, because of the way I stormed out of his house after the football game. She'd spent a lot of time pondering her actions and as much as that quarrel had hurt both of them, Quinn knew she had done the right thing. For the first time in a relationship, she recognized what her boundaries were. She knew what kind of behavior she would accept and what she wouldn't. *And even better, I articulated it to him.* Their relationship had grown since the night Caden arrived to apologize. She smiled. *Even without the passionate sex that marked our first weeks together.*

They met for dinner once a week, sampling restaurants in southern New Hampshire. Most of the time, it was just the two of them, but once, Danny and Brooke and Robbie and Jen joined them. The evening was full of belly laughs as the three men told tales of shenanigans they pulled in high school. Quinn felt like she had a fuller picture of Caden and loved that he had such strong friendships.

Brooke and Jen invited her to join them at a spa weekend in March, when the boys would be off for a weekend of college basketball. Caden had offered to cancel those plans, but Quinn refused to let him do that. She was always mindful of how co-dependent she had been in other relationships, and she suspected that might have been true for Caden and Mary. She would not abandon her female friendships for a man and didn't want him ignoring his friends.

Every night, they talked long past Quinn's usual bedtime, learning more about each other, sharing what their days had been like, and arousing each other the same way they had when Caden first started calling. Now it was Valentine's Day and Quinn was excited to spend two nights in his arms again. They had planned a special weekend, and she couldn't wait to get it started.

She stood at the window watching for him and had the door open before he was halfway across the parking lot. Caden's eyes raked her body and grew dark with desire. She was wearing black leggings and a red V-neck sweater. He reached out and stroked the sweater. "So soft," he murmured. "I've missed you." Bending, he kissed the pulse point on her neck.

Laughter bubbled up in Quinn. "It's only been three days since we had dinner together." Desire quickly overtook the laughter, and she melted against him. Her voice was husky with want as she said, "I've missed you, too." Her hands rubbed his back, bringing him closer to her, and she could feel how much he wanted her.

Caden sighed. "I thought we agreed to delay gratification tonight. That we would eat first." He continued to hold her tightly.

Quinn groaned. "Must you be so practical?" She separated from him and headed to the kitchen.

They were almost finished eating when Caden reached for her hand. "I love you. I'm so excited to spend forty-eight hours with you. That ski trip was eons ago."

"Me too," Quinn murmured. While he cleared the table, she made Irish Coffee, took it to the living room and started a fire. When she turned from the fireplace, Caden was waiting on the couch, ready for her to snuggle against him, which she happily did. Sipping the coffee, they chatted softly. "Do you still want to find a time for Danny and Robbie and the girls to come up?" They had considered inviting them to come up for this weekend.

"I do if you do. It probably won't be until April since you'll be going to Maine again and we have the trip to Florida." His legs were stretched in front of him, and Quinn placed her palm on his thigh. He placed his hand on top of hers. "I'm glad it's just us this weekend. I don't want to share you with anyone."

"Mmmm, I feel the same way." Her hand slid along his thigh, and she enjoyed watching him squirm, trying to make room in his jeans for the erection she knew was there. Softly, she feathered her fingers over the bulge.

"You're killing me," he whispered. "Have we delayed gratification long enough?" He leaned his head down to nibble on her neck.

Quinn increased the pressure on his cock. "Let me finish my coffee." She looked at him with mischief in her eyes.

"Mine's done." He leaned forward, clattering the mug onto the coffee table. His now empty hand slid under Quinn's sweater and up to her bra, where he lazily traced circles along the lace.

Quinn struggled to stay still, watching his eyes have the same mischievous challenge in them that hers did.

Caden leaned down and gently kissed her lips. "So glad Danny and Rob aren't here." His fingers moved under the band of her bra, reaching up to her nipple, which instantly pebbled.

Quinn gave in to the squirming, trying unsuccessfully to increase the pressure of his touch. Finally, she said, "I'm done," and placed her mug on the coffee table. Standing, she moved to the stairs with Caden following behind.

He grabbed his bag before climbing the stairs and when they reached Quinn's bedroom, he placed it beside the bed, then wrapped his arms tightly around her, releasing the passion he'd been holding back. His fingers tangled in her hair and his kisses, which had been so gentle earlier, were hungry now.

Quinn reached for the hem of his sweater, and he let her pull it off. She trailed kisses all the way to his pants, then went back to his nipple. Her tongue circled it before she raked it with her teeth. The sounds Caden was making told her he was feeling the same sensations she was.

He let her play for a few minutes, then tugged her sweater off and pushed her bra out of the way so he could get at her breasts. He sucked and nibbled at the nub. Raising his head to look at her, he said, "Do you know how hard it's been to sit in a restaurant having dinner with you when all I can think about is how much I want to touch you? How much I want you touching me. We can't go a month again."

"Never again." She reached for the waistband of his jeans.

"Wait." Caden grabbed her hands. "I've got something for you." He moved his bag to the bed and rummaged inside until he found a rectangular box that he handed to Quinn. "Let's sit." He grinned. "It's actually for both of us."

Quinn took it warily and lifted the top off. There, cradled in foam, was a nugget of silicone with narrow arms protruding from the sides. She gingerly lifted it out, rolling it between her fingers, thoroughly inspecting it. "Is this a...?" She looked at Caden, feeling even hotter than when they were going at each other. "A vibrator?"

"It is." His eyes twinkled at her. "I overheard an intern talking about it and I was intrigued." He took it out of her hands. "The arms wrap around my cock. It's supposed to prolong things. And the body should hit right on your clit."

Quinn's face flushed and the moisture between her thighs increased. "Vibes have always been a solitary thing for me." She put her hand over his. "I'm intrigued too. Although if my orgasms get any stronger, I'll probably perish."

"I'll revive you. Wanna try it out?" He stood up and unzipped his jeans.

Quinn nodded and joined him in removing the rest of her clothes before lying on the bed and beckoning for him to join her.

They kissed, and Caden's hand reached between her legs. "You're drenched. Does that mean you like this idea?"

Her answer was to pull a condom out of the box and sheathe his pulsing cock. Caden reached for the vibrator, and Quinn said, "Let me." Giggling, she spread the arms and wrapped them around his cock. "Where should it be?"

Caden shrugged.

"And how tight? I don't want to break you." She spread her legs, inviting him in.

"We'll have to experiment." Caden climbed on top and caressed her body, making sure she was ready.

"Umm. Lots of experimentation. I like that idea" She reached out and guided his cock into her. The vibrating bulb hit exactly the spot Quinn preferred. "Holy God. You might last longer, but I'm not going to." Her legs wrapped around his waist, bringing him deep inside. As he plunged in and out, more than one orgasm washed over her. "Cade, oh Cade, don't stop." When he finally came, Quinn felt like a bowl of limp noodles.

"Holy God is right." Caden's breath was finally returning to normal. "I don't know if it was the vibrator or how much I missed you, but that was fucking amazing."

Quinn propped herself up on an elbow, held her hand out to show him how she was trembling. "I may never get off this bed. 'Vibrator with a partner', a bucket list item I didn't even know I wanted."

"It was a first for me, too." He kissed her. "Just in case you were wondering."

Chapter Twelve

A Night In The Guesthouse

Quinn

SUNSHINE STREAMING THROUGH THE window awoke Quinn, and she reached across the bed, finding it empty. Caden strolled in with two cups of coffee. "Hey sleepy head, it's almost eight. Did I wear you out?"

"Something like that." She reached for one of the mugs. They had made love twice more during the night. "Come sit with me. If you can control yourself."

"I'll be a good boy." Caden crawled under the covers beside her. "Until tonight."

They sat in companionable silence, with Quinn leaning against him. "This is nice. But we should get up. Our class is at ten."

"Take a left here." Quinn was directing Caden to the King Arthur Baking School. She'd taken classes there and thought it would be fun for them to do together. They were going to make rustic fruit tarts.

They were given aprons as soon as they walked in and then sat for an introduction to the alchemy of pie dough. There were eight people in the class, and Caden was the only man. They measured, sifted, mixed, then rolled out the dough. Caden selected apples for his filling and Quinn appreciated watching him peel them. He was steady and sure with the paring knife, and she wondered if that came from his training as a surgeon. *He would have been amazing.* She'd had that thought several times since he had shared on New Year's Day that he started out as a surgeon. *He's amazing at everything.*

Quinn filled her tart with raspberries and while the tarts baked, they walked across the courtyard to the store. She had shopped there several times and always spent more money than she planned on.

Caden's head was on a swivel, looking at all the mixes and the baking items. "Wow, I didn't even know some of these things existed. My mother would go wild in here. I'm surprised Claire never brought her." He had told his mom about the class, and she told him while she'd heard of King Arthur, she'd never been there.

"She could come up to visit Claire some weekend and we could bring her here."

"I don't know about that." Caden shook his head. "I don't want to share you. We have little enough time as it is."

Quinn added some scone mixes to her cart and thought for a minute. "Do you think she'd like to take a class? They do them during the week. She and I could take one on my day off. I'd like to get to know her better."

"She'd love that."

The tarts came out beautifully, and they were given decorated sugar cookies for Valentine's Day. They dropped Quinn's tart at her townhouse, then drove to downtown Hanover to wander through the shops before driving to the guest house to spend the night. Caden picked up a "Hanover" T-shirt at the Dartmouth Bookstore, resisting Quinn's attempts to have him buy a "Dartmouth" one. "I can't wear a shirt from a college other than Boston University."

"College was ten years ago," she teased.

"Doesn't matter. I'm loyal to my alma mater. Aren't you?"

"My closet contains nothing from my time in Virginia." Her answer was short, and she didn't elaborate. Hoping to change the direction of their conversation, Quinn led him into Java Junction. "They have amazing hot chocolate and pastries here."

With mugs of hot chocolate and cupcakes in hand, they found a table in the corner of the crowded cafe. Quinn contemplated her red velvet cupcake with cream cheese frosting. "It's too pretty to eat." She took a sip of the hot chocolate and sighed.

Caden touched his finger to her lip. "You've got whipped cream right there. I'd lick it off, but who knows where that would lead." As Quinn wiped her mouth, he continued, "I'll have no problem eating this. I love chocolate and peanut butter." He took a bite and moaned. "Delicious."

A large, noisy group entered, and Quinn raised her hand in greeting as she picked Izzy out of the throng. Izzy's eyes lit up when she saw Quinn, and as she shook her blond curls free from a knit headband she touched the arm of the boy next to her, then walked toward Quinn and Caden's table. "Happy Valentine's Day!" Her mouth curved in an impish smile.

"And the same to you," Quinn said. "Cade, this is Isabella Wiley, my swimming partner and honorary little sister. Izzy, this is Caden Brady."

"Nice to meet you, Izzy." Caden extended his hand. "Quinn tells me you give her a good challenge in the pool."

"Not good enough yet, but that day is coming." Izzy shook his hand. "You treat her right. She's a special lady."

"No worries there. I'm well aware of how special she is."

Quinn blushed and said, "Is that the elusive Ethan who pulled you back here early?"

"Yes, and I can't abandon him for too long." Izzy leaned down to hug Quinn and whispered in her ear. "Mama Mia, he *is* hot!" Without giving Quinn a chance to reply, she returned to her friends.

Quinn shook her head. "She's incorrigible."

"I'm glad you have friends who look out for you."

They were almost finished when Ashley walked by the cafe. Seeing Quinn, she changed direction and entered the shop. She pulled out a chair at their table, making herself comfortable. Before Quinn could say anything, Ashley said, "You must be Caden. I've heard a lot about you. I'm Ashley. Her only friend who likes football."

Caden grinned. "Your name has come up frequently. It's good to have a face to go with the name."

"Indeed, it is. Can you guys stay a while? Seeing the remnants of your cupcakes makes me want one, and the line isn't too bad." Ashley stood and said, "I have news," before she walked to the counter.

"As you can see, none of my friends are shy."

"They complement you well. This is fun. I enjoy seeing where you hang out and meeting your friends."

Ashley returned, carrying three mugs and a cupcake. "There's always room for more hot chocolate." She sat down and took a long sip of her drink. "Ahhh, it's so good. How's your weekend been so far?"

Quinn noticed the gleam in Ashley's eyes. "It's been wonderful. But you first, what's your news?"

Ashley extended her left hand with a wide smile. "I'm engaged!"

Quinn squealed and jumped up from her chair to hug Ashley. "When? How? I need all the details. I'm so happy for you!"

"We went to the Hanover Inn for dinner and just before dessert arrived, Aaron got down on one knee and popped the question. We've talked about marriage, but this came totally out of the blue."

Quinn looked at Caden, watching them with a smile. She thought his eyes held a hint of sadness. "This is a big deal."

"Of course it is." He turned toward Ashley. "Congratulations. Getting engaged is exciting."

"It was, it is. We're going to Connecticut tomorrow to tell my parents."

"Oh my God." Quinn laughed. "Your mother is going to lose her mind."

Ashley nodded, then explained to Caden. "I'm the only girl in my family. I have three brothers, all married. My mother will go nuts because she'll be included in my wedding planning."

"No small intimate affair for you?"

"Unlikely."

The three of them chatted as they enjoyed their drinks. "Good luck tomorrow." Quinn hugged Ashley. "Your parents will be thrilled. Aaron is such a good guy."

Caden opened the door to the guesthouse, and as he reached for Quinn's coat, said, "I'm glad you were okay with spending one of our nights here."

"Are you kidding? I love it here. It's like going on a mini vacation for me. And you said you were going to cook."

"You don't want to eat now, do you? It's kind of soon after that cupcake."

"Do you have something else in mind?"

"I do. I need about ten minutes. Can you put in your earbuds while you wait?" When he came back, he found Quinn stretched out on the couch with her eyes closed. He bent to kiss her. "Wake up, Sleeping Beauty."

"I wasn't asleep," she murmured as they walked into the bedroom where several red pillar candles were lighting the room, and a red satin robe lay on the bed. "Wow."

"Happy Valentine's Day, part two. Your clothes have to come off for the rest. Can I help with that?"

Quinn smiled. Caden unbuttoned her white shirt, then pulled the red camisole gently over her head. He unhooked her bra, picked up the robe, and held it while she slid her arms in.

Moving to her jeans, Quinn remained still while he undid the zipper and shoved them to the ground. He held her hand as she stepped over the pile on the floor. His fingers moved to her thong, hesitating on the lace. He was being very restrained, and Quinn wasn't sure where his actions were leading, but she could read the desire in his eyes and knew it was as strong as hers. He slid the thong to the floor and kneeled to remove her socks.

He stood and wrapped his arms around Quinn, stroking her back. The satin felt rich against her skin, and when Caden released her, they both sighed. "We'll get to that in a bit," he said. "Come with me." They walked to the bathroom, where the tub was waiting, full of bubbles sprinkled with red rose petals. More candles provided the lighting.

Quinn's hand went over her mouth. "This looks positively decadent."

"That was the idea." He slid the robe off and watched as she sank into the bubbles. Just as he had done back in December, he sat on the bench next to her. "My gift of a vibrator looks kind of lame next to Ashley's engagement ring."

"I love the vibrator. It's absolutely perfect." Her hand came out of the bubbles to clasp his. "Was it hard for you to see her excitement?"

"A little. It brought back the night I proposed to Mary." He ran his free hand through his hair. "Don't get me wrong. I still firmly believe in marriage. It just stirred up something."

Quinn squeezed his hand.

"If we're going to get into true confessions, can I ask why you have nothing from your time in Virginia? I know your first year was rough, but you stayed. It can't have been all bad."

"Actually, it was." Quinn sank deeper into the bubbles. "Do you remember me telling you on Christmas Eve that I was involved with someone I only saw twice a week?" When he nodded, she smiled. "Of course you do. I was with him for more than three years and for almost all of that time, he was involved with someone else." She scoffed and looked at Caden. "He had a baby with her. And I was oblivious. When I left Richmond, I wanted no reminders."

Caden stroked her hair. "Oh babe, I'm so sorry. I really didn't intend to get into such heavy topics. I'll be right back." When he returned, he was carrying two wine glasses. He handed one to Quinn and touched his glass to hers. "To finding the right people." They both sipped the wine, then he said, "Let's switch to a happier topic. You said you take a trip every summer."

Quinn nodded.

"Can I come with you this year?"

Quinn smiled. "I'd love that. But...I'm usually gone for two weeks."

"Two weeks exploring with you sounds like heaven. Do you know where you want to go?"

"I haven't even thought about it. This handsome doctor I met has distracted me."

Caden smiled. "Have you been to France? I've always wanted to go there."

"I haven't, and it's definitely somewhere I want to go." The water was cooling, and she stood to climb out. Caden dried her and wrapped the robe around her. As they walked back to the bedroom, she said, "I'd really like you to show me Ireland. Would you like to go back there?" Caden's eyes lit up, and Quinn knew he liked her idea.

"I'd love to show you Ireland. Maybe we can do both. A week in Ireland and a week in Paris."

Quinn put her arms around him. "These are some serious long-term plans we're making."

"They sure are." Caden held her tightly. "I love it. And I love you."

Chapter Thirteen

Caden's Panic Attack

Quinn

NEAR THE END OF February, Quinn groaned as she looked out at the foot of snow that had fallen overnight. *Why now? We're almost done with winter!* She sent Caden a text.

Quinn: Three weeks until Florida. I can't wait! I'm brushing a foot of snow off my car this morning.

He sent back sunshine and palm tree emojis.

Their relationship had flourished in the time since Valentine's Day. Quinn traveled to Boston when she had a day off and they started planning their summer trip. Sam had texted a few times, and she was happy that he was making strides toward getting his life together.

On Tuesday, a reminder popped up on her phone, letting her know it was time to schedule her annual exam. It was nearly March, and a decision needed to be made about birth control. She was certain an IUD would be the way to go.

At home, she went online to set up an appointment, and the paperwork wanted the date of her last period. Studying her tracker, she realized it had been December twenty-sixth. She should have had a period at the end of January. *Holy shit. I'm late. Not just a day or two late—almost a month!* Her face flushed as her heart began beating wildly. *Am I pregnant?* They had been careful, always using a condom. She did the math. If she was pregnant, it would have happened during the ski trip, when she was ovulating. Which meant she could be six weeks pregnant. The symptoms of pregnancy—sore breasts, nausea, and fatigue—often started by the fifth week, and she didn't have any of those.

Better to be safe, though. Quinn threw on her coat, grabbed her keys, drove to the pharmacy, and purchased two pregnancy tests, knowing whatever the result, she probably wouldn't believe it.

Back home, she hurried to the bathroom, took the test, and waited for the prescribed time by pacing around the town house. The result was negative, and waves of relief poured over her, tinged with disappointment. She decided she'd wait twenty-four hours before taking the other one. Sleep was elusive as she tossed and turned all night, considering what a pregnancy might mean.

The prospect of having Caden's baby didn't distress her. The idea actually excited her. Her only misgiving was about how he would feel. Early on, he had mentioned not wanting an unplanned baby, but that was after their first time together. She felt very secure in his love and thought he'd be happy about having a baby with her.

All the next day, her mind wandered, trying to think of reasons for being so late if she wasn't pregnant. Online research gave her a couple of plausible explanations, but nothing definitive.

The second test still gave her a negative result.

Caden was coming up for the weekend, and she would tell him then she was late but not pregnant and ask if his medical knowledge gave him any ideas about why. She imagined them laughing in relief at her not being pregnant.

Maybe we'll have a discussion about children. She was more than ready for that.

Caden

It was a frigid weekend, and Quinn and Caden never left the townhouse. They both had studying to do, and after it was done, they spent the rest of Saturday in bed, watching movies.

Caden was up first on Sunday. He built a fire and made pancakes and bacon for breakfast. When Quinn walked downstairs, she found a blanket on the floor in front of the fireplace and the food ready for an indoor picnic.

When they finished eating, Quinn picked up the dishes and asked him to sit on the couch with her. He joined her and put his arm over her shoulder, pulling her tight to him, loving the feel of her. "What's up?"

Quinn hesitated before she answered, and he looked at her expectantly. "I'm late."

Caden grinned. "Late for…" Realization hit him, and without warning, pictures from the Natick bedroom started flashing in his mind. He recoiled from Quinn, backing up as far as he could on the couch. *Pregnant? How could she be pregnant? We used a condom every time.* He knew a condom wasn't foolproof, but they'd been so careful.

His heart pounded in his chest. *She's fucked around with someone else.* His ears began ringing. He looked toward Quinn, and she was talking, but he couldn't hear her words. *It's Sam. She's fucking Sam!* He tried to take a breath, but felt like no air was getting into his lungs.

"Caden. I'm pretty certain I'm not pregnant." She reached for his hand, looking alarmed. "Caden, talk to me."

He snatched his hand away and struggled to his feet. Gasping for breath, he stumbled toward the door, and Quinn followed. He raised one hand and shook his head. She stopped, and Caden opened the door. He tried to say, "Give me a minute," but couldn't speak. Instead, he walked outside, slamming the door behind him.

He was bent over, hands on his knees, struggling to breathe, when he heard Quinn open the door. He was wearing sweatpants with a long-sleeved tee and was barefoot, standing on the snow-packed walkway, but he didn't feel the cold.

"My God, what is going on? You're going to freeze," she called to him. "Cade, you need to come back in. It's below zero out there."

He straightened and rubbed the back of his neck. He stiffened momentarily when he saw Quinn, and he was still struggling to pull in enough oxygen.

"Caden, please come in," Quinn begged.

He plodded toward her and slowly climbed the stairs leading inside. Quinn shut the door behind him and took his hand. He was shaking, and he let her lead him to the fireplace. "Sit here." He sank to the floor, and she pulled a blanket from the couch to wrap around him.

Quinn put more wood on the fire, and after a few moments, she dropped to the floor next to him. He was still trembling, and she rubbed his feet through the blanket.

Without looking at him, she said, "I don't think I'm pregnant. I took a test, actually two tests, both negative. And I don't have any symptoms." Her voice became unsteady. "Wh-what's going on, Caden?" She turned and looked into his eyes.

Caden tried to speak, but no words came.

"Is this what you were talking about when you mentioned panic attacks?"

Caden took a deep breath. His heart was still racing, but his breath was coming more normally. "Yes." He took another breath. "I heard you say you were late, and the bedroom in Natick started flashing. I know you said more than that, but I couldn't hear it. You and Mary were all jumbled up in my mind." His voice broke.

"Was it like this the other times? Outside of the hospital, I've never seen anyone react like you just did." She brought her hand to her mouth and tapped her lips. "You scared me."

Caden wrapped his arms around her. "God, I never want to do that. This was much more extreme than the other two times. Before, it was the heart pounding, the ringing in my ears, and gasping for air. This time—there were thoughts." He shook his head, trying to clear his mind. "Thoughts I don't want to have."

"What kind of thoughts?"

Caden stared into the distance.

Quinn extricated herself from his arms and gazed into his eyes. "I've been honest with you. Brutally honest, according to your description. I need you to do the same."

Caden sighed. "I don't want to hurt you."

"You'll hurt me more by not sharing what's going on. I'm a big girl. I can take it."

"We've been careful. I thought... if you were pregnant, it must mean you'd been with someone else. It must mean you'd been with..."

"Sam."

Caden's face crumpled in pain. "Yeah." He ran his hand through his hair. "But you must understand, I don't really think that. I *know* you wouldn't be with him, or anyone, but the thought was pounding in my brain with the pictures of Mary in bed with that rando." He swallowed hard. "And this was a new twist—I could hear Danny saying, as he read the journals New Year's morning, 'My God, Cade, she's been fucking around since two years into your relationship.'"

Quinn's face was pale. "I don't know what to say. You talk to your therapist about all of this?"

"I have been since December." He pulled Quinn close to him again, and they sat in silence for several minutes.

Finally, Caden spoke again. He had to fix this. "Do you believe me? That I don't really think you've been with anyone else? I know if you're pregnant, it's mine."

Quinn nodded slowly. "I believe you. But the subconscious thoughts scare me. You being so tied up in your head that you'd go out into the snow barefoot... scares me."

"I know, I know."

"I love you." Quinn caressed his cheek. "I want us to get through this together."

Caden nodded.

"Have you warmed up? I'm going to get us another cup of coffee."

When Quinn came back with the coffee, Caden had put another log on the fire and moved to the couch. She sat beside him, and they were quiet again until Caden said, "No symptoms? Two negative tests? You're probably not pregnant."

"I don't think so."

He put a hand on her belly. "I wouldn't be upset if you were."

"Really?"

"It wouldn't exactly be the timing I envisioned, but I love the idea of our baby growing in you. I've thought about it since the first time I saw you holding Rory."

She smiled. "That's exactly how I felt when I realized how late I was, and I hoped you'd agree. I was a little disappointed by the negative test. I've thought about having your baby since I met Rory, too."

He frowned. "I don't know why you'd be this late. My obstetrics rotation focused more on delivery, not much on women's health."

"My annual is in two weeks, and I'll figure it out. I'm going to go with an IUD again."

He held her and said, "We'll decide together when the time is right for a baby. I can't wait for that. I love you so much."

Quinn

Caden knocked on Quinn's door on Friday night, and she opened it with a big grin, as she always did. She drew him into a hug, but he held back for a moment before wrapping his arms around her. He buried his face in her hair.

After Caden had left the Sunday before, Quinn had tried to reconcile the warm conversation they'd had about having a baby with the distraught Caden who had stumbled out into the snow. She'd spent a long-time online researching PTRS and panic attacks, but didn't find any answers.

They always went directly to the bedroom after a week apart, but instead he led her to the living room, where they sat on the couch.

Quinn's radar went into high gear. *Something's wrong.* "What's going on? Where's your bag?"

"I'm not staying." Caden's voice was serious.

"What do you mean? Is something wrong with your family? Is someone sick?"

"No, no one is sick. Unless you count me." He sighed. "I've had a lot of time to think this week, and I can't do this, Quinn."

"Can't do... what?"

"This. Us. I can't be with you anymore."

"You're breaking up with me?" Her heart raced, and she felt like she might throw up. "Why? We spent last weekend talking about babies. We love each other. What is wrong with you?"

"Quinn, I was out of control and on the verge of being abusive last Sunday." He looked broken. "I won't be that kind of man. It's not me, and I can't risk it happening again."

"It wasn't abuse. You'd never hurt me. We'll figure it out. I won't do…"

"Won't do what, Quinn?" he asked quietly. "You did nothing wrong. Nothing. You can't live your life trying not to trigger me when we don't even know what those triggers are. What if I had hit you? Would you be okay with that?"

Quinn drew back. "No, but you didn't hit me. You wouldn't hit me."

He shook his head. "I don't know what I'll do the next time. I won't let you put up with that."

"You get to decide what I put up with?" Her voice shook with anger.

"No, I don't, but I can decide about the situations I'm in, and I will not be in one where I abuse a woman."

She put a hand on his arm. "It's a sickness. If you had cancer, would you be walking away from me? I *love* you, and I want us to find the answer to this together."

"I've been going to therapy once a week since the first attack back in December, and it's done no good, because what happened last week was far worse." He clenched his hands into fists. "I don't know how to fix this, and I will not risk hurting you more."

She struggled to hold back sobs. "So, are you going to live out your life alone? Not letting yourself love anyone? Because you and I are good together. You're good for me. You showed me what it's like to be truly loved and cared for, and I think I did the same for you. Do you think you're going to find someone better?"

"No, I don't." His certainty was heartbreaking. "I won't find anyone else who rocks my world like you do, but I love you too much to let you settle for less than you deserve. I'm damaged, and you need someone who is whole."

"You can't do this." She gripped his arm. "It makes no sense!"

Caden shook his arm free, took a deep breath, and said, "Yes, it does, and in time, you'll realize this is the only way." He rose to leave.

She stood and reached for him, but he moved away.

"No!" she gasped.

He paused at the door. "Goodbye, Quinn. I love you."

She walked to the window to watch him as he left, trembling with disbelief and pain.

Caden

Caden climbed into his car, dragging the door shut, then taking out his phone to look at two numbers, Ashley's and Sam's. Quinn had put Ashley's number in his phone several weeks earlier, telling him if he ever couldn't get in touch with her, to try Ashley. He'd memorized Sam's number from her phone and added it to his contacts, not knowing why.

But now he did. He didn't want Quinn to be alone, and he knew both would be willing and able to go to her.

Ashley and I only met once. They are close, but she's also a colleague. If I call her, will this become breakroom talk tomorrow? I wouldn't want that, and I know Quinn wouldn't either. I'm sure she'll tell Ashley, but it needs to be on her terms.

He drew in a shaky breath and blew it out. A tear escaped his eye, and he squeezed his eyes closed, trying to regain the control he'd kept while talking to Quinn.

So, it's going to be Sam.

> Caden: Hey, Sam, this is Caden. I just ended things with Quinn, and I think she could really use a friend.

> Sam: WTF, how'd you get my number?

> Caden: From Quinn's phone. Please be a friend to her.

> Sam: Anything for Quinn, man. What happened?

> Caden: She can tell you if she wants to. She can tell you all of it. Thanks.

He drove away with the tears he'd worked so hard to hold back streaming down his cheeks.

Chapter Fourteen

Caden Changes His Will

Mid May

Caden

CADEN EMERGED FROM THE subway, blinking as the setting sun assaulted his eyes. He started the short walk to Robbie and Jen's house in Somerville. It was a warm May evening and as he walked by a lilac bush in full bloom, the scent overwhelmed him. *Quinn would love this. We never came to Somerville. She never saw Robbie's house.* Thoughts like that crossed his mind every day, sometimes more than once a day. At first, they had overwhelmed him, but now, after two months of therapy and a regular regimen of anti-anxiety meds, he was merely sad. And he allowed himself to feel the sadness instead of running away from it.

He'd done a lot of running the first six weeks, upping his nights on the Medico van from one a week to four, hoping that working on the van after a full day at the hospital would exhaust him. In an effort to get out of his head, he visited the waterfront encampment every week trying unsuccessfully to convince Marty to reenter the world where they both knew he belonged. Ned never came back. He went from the hospital to a shelter and a social worker there found he had a sister living in Maine whom he had lost touch with years earlier. She was grateful to be reunited with him and insisted he move to her house. Caden counted that as a win in a year that, so far, had too few.

But ten-thirty found him wide awake every night staring at his phone, resisting the urge to call or text Quinn. The first couple of weeks she sent a text every day, often multiple texts, and he ignored them. Lately, she was only sending one a week, but it was always at ten-thirty.

He knew the sessions with Jean were helping. Sleep was coming easier and colleagues at the hospital were no longer approaching him with trepidation the way they had right after he left Quinn. He was emerging from the fog he'd been in and two weeks ago, he'd joined Danny and Robbie at O'Malley's for the first time since February. *But I'll never know if I'm over those panic attacks because I'm never going to see her again.* His heart grew cold, the same way it did every time he thought about never seeing Quinn. *I will not risk it.*

Caden bounded up the stairs and knocked on Robbie's door. Hearing Robbie's voice telling him the door was open, he walked in to find him and Jenny tidying the kitchen. He kissed her on the cheek. "It's good to see you."

"Twice in less than a week." Caden had attended a Red Sox game with them the Saturday before. "It's nice. We've missed you."

"I know. Are you going to make it on Saturday?" Caden had invited them as well as Danny and Brooke to dinner. He had something he needed to tell them.

"We wouldn't miss it. Dining on your rooftop terrace is one of the joys of summer."

"I'm sorry to take the big guy away from you tonight. I won't take up much of his time."

"It's okay, I've got a bubble bath calling my name." Jen headed upstairs, leaving Caden and Robbie in the kitchen.

A bubble bath. Pictures of Quinn at the guest house on Valentine's Day, submerged in bubbles with rose petals scattered on top, flooded his mind. Caden squeezed his eyes shut, trying to displace them.

"Caden." Robbie tapped his shoulder. "Should we go to my study? You said you need some legal help. Am I going to need to take notes?"

Caden nodded. "The study sounds good. What I need is short and sweet. You won't need notes."

Robbie's study had deep hunter green walls with dark woodwork. Shelves holding his law books lined two walls, and a large desk sat in the corner. Caden sank down into one of the brown leather chairs while Robbie poured them each a shot of Irish whiskey. "Turning me onto Jameson's may be one of the worst things you ever did to me. I had a hell of a headache Sunday morning."

Caden smiled. "Yeah, me too. Not sure it was just the whiskey, though. The beers consumed may have contributed as well." He ran his hand through his hair. "How are things on the baby-making front? Still no luck?"

Robbie studied him before answering. "Is that what you came here for? To ask me if Jenny's pregnant? If you hadn't completely disappeared on us for two months, you'd know she isn't."

Caden knew that his withdrawal from their lives had hurt his friends and Robbie's tone reflected that. He was surprised they didn't give him crap about it when he rejoined them at O'Malley's.

"I'm sorry. I wasn't fit company for anyone, not even myself. And I'm sorry, she's not pregnant yet. I know how much you both want a child."

"Yeah, it's rough." Robbie's tone softened. "It hasn't been a year yet, so if she questions her doctor, the answer is always to just keep trying. That Brooke gets pregnant just by Danny looking at her doesn't make it any easier." Brooke and Danny had a baby due in October. "But seriously, that's not why we're sitting in my study, is it?"

"No. I'm going to Honduras for two months to work at a medical mission. I leave in a couple of weeks." Caden could see the surprise on Robbie's face. "It's why I invited you all for dinner on Saturday. I'm going to tell the others then."

"Whoa, I was not expecting you to tell me that. How come I'm so privileged to find out first?"

"I.... I want to change my will...."

Robbie cut him off. "That's not my area of expertise."

"I know, I know, just hear me out. What I want is simple. I'd rather not use my usual lawyer, and I don't have time to find another one and meet with them before I leave. I'm hoping if I tell you what I want, that there's someone at your firm who can take care of it for me."

"We have a division for estate planning." He reached for a pad of paper. "I definitely need to make some notes."

"No, you really don't. I want to leave everything to Quinn."

Robbie shook his head. "You want to do what?"

"I want a will that leaves everything I have, to Quinn."

"What about your family?"

"What about them? Robbie, we all have far more money than any of us will ever need."

"Everything? The brownstone, the Beemer? Is where you're going dangerous? I mean, are you likely to get killed? Jesus Cade!"

"No, not all that dangerous, but planning for this made me think. I could walk across the street and get hit by a bus. I've been considering this for a while and now's the time to do it."

"Are you going to tell her?"

He shook his head. "I'm not...I'm not in communication with her. Likely nothing will happen to me, and she'll never even know. If something happens, I'm sure you'll be able to explain it to her."

Robbie sat for several minutes, rolling the shot glass between his hands. "Cade, why not? It's obvious how much you care about her. You're talking about giving her millions of dollars."

Caden walked over to the bar and refilled his shot glass. He knocked back the whiskey before he turned to Robbie. "I can't. You don't understand. You don't know what I did."

"So, tell me, make me understand. Jenny thinks we have some kind of bro code going on because when she asks how you are, I tell her I don't know. She doesn't believe that you haven't told Danny and me anything. What happened Cade? We used to share every detail of our lives."

Caden picked up the bottle of whiskey and started walking toward Robbie, then stopped and pivoted back to the bar where he put the alcohol down and picked up two bottles of water. He sank back down into the leather chair and tossed one to Robbie before taking a long swallow. "When I see Quinn with another man, or I even think about her with another man, pictures of Mary riding that rando flash in my head. My ears ring and I can't breathe. I lose my mind."

Robbie pondered his words, then said, "You know how often I've seen PTSD proposed as a defense and how overused I think it is, so I don't say this lightly, but that's what it sounds like is happening to you."

"It is. I know it is, but I don't know how to make it stop."

"Aren't you seeing a therapist?"

"Twice a week since February."

"Quinn would understand. She'd help you work through it."

"No!" Caden ran his hand through his hair. "I ended it, and it needs to stay ended."

"When have you seen her with another guy? It was obvious to all of us how much in love with you she was. She'd never look at another guy."

"With Danny at the New Year's Eve party."

"Danny? Dude, we all dance with each other. That's harmless. Does Danny know?"

"I was dancing with Brooke, so she saw my reaction and yes, she told him."

"And that's why you ended it?"

"It's not a onetime thing. And it's escalated. The week before I broke it off, she told me she was late, and I flipped out. The pictures of Mary started flashing, and I could hear Danny telling me she'd been screwing around the whole time we were together. I was wild with the idea that Quinn was having sex with someone else, probably her friend Sam. I walked outside to try to get myself under control. Barefoot, in the snow." He paused, took a long swallow of the water and looked toward the ceiling. He looked back at Robbie. "I was right at the edge of going at her physically and I won't be that man. Won't be someone who abuses a woman."

"You and Quinn can conquer it together."

He shook his head. "No, I don't trust myself." He finished the water. "Can you help me? Please? I'll always love her and there's no one else I want to leave the fruits of my grandfather's labor to."

Robbie nodded. "Yeah, I can call in a couple of favors to get it done in the next week. Someone will call you for the details they'll need to get it written." He put the water bottle down. "I had no idea what prompted the breakup. I'm sorry you weren't comfortable sharing that with us."

Caden ran his hand through his hair. "I know. You won't believe this." He laughed. "Outside of my therapist, the only person I've 'talked' to is Sam. He texted me after Quinn told him the whole story and we've been texting off and on since then. Weird, huh?"

Robbie nodded. "Kinda."

"I'm marginally better, coping, I guess. I'm hoping this mission trip will get me out of my head." He stood up. "I'll get out of your hair. Your beautiful wife is waiting for you, fresh from a bubble bath. You can share this with her, tell her there's no bro code."

Back at the brownstone, Caden stepped onto the terrace, allowing the memory of being out there with Quinn to wash over him. *She was here so little and yet she's everywhere.* For the first time in his life, the city he loved no longer brought him joy. Nothing brought him joy. He stretched out on the lounger and thought back a few weeks. He'd flown to North Carolina to visit Cathleen. After their dinner in January, Caden had made it a point to check in with her regularly. Even after he left Quinn and was isolating himself from friends and family, he continued to text her. School was done and she was preparing to leave.

Cathleen had picked him up at the airport and when he saw her car, he laughed for the first time in weeks. She had climbed out and doing her best Vanna White impersonation, said, "What do you think?" It was a brand-new silver Volvo SUV.

The last car Caden had seen her drive was a ten-year-old red Toyota. "Nice. Quite an upgrade." Her birthday had been three weeks earlier, meaning she now had access to her trust fund.

"I know I'm fulfilling every cliché in the book by rushing out to buy a luxury car." She grinned. "But I'd had Ruby since high school. It was time and I'm going to be living in snow country..."

"You don't have to convince me Cath." He continued chuckling as he hoisted his bag into the backseat. "My BMW is just as clichéd."

They spent two days packing her belongings. "This went faster than I thought it would. It's been a big help having you here." They were sitting at an outside restaurant having burgers and beer. "I wasn't planning to start the drive north until Thursday, but we can start tomorrow if you want."

"I'm not in any rush to get back." The tension he'd carried since that night in Hanover was receding. Neither of them had talked about their personal lives and he was fine with that.

"I could show you around tomorrow. Want to try rowing?"

"Sure. Are you going to continue after you move?"

"I think so. I've seen rowers on that river between New Hampshire and Vermont. There must be a club."

"The Connecticut River." Caden chuckled but inwardly, mention of the boundary between the states sparked memories of Quinn. *But they're not hitting as hard here as they do in Boston.*

The next morning, Cathleen drove Caden on a tour of the city, pointing out favorite places and touring the campus of the university before going to the club after lunch. "I usually row in the evening but this will be better. There won't be many people here."

The man behind the counter greeted them enthusiastically. "I thought you were already gone. Didn't you say it was your last time when you were here Friday?"

"Hey John. Yes, but packing took less time than I thought. This is my brother Caden. He came to help, and he'll make the drive home with me. We're leaving tomorrow."

Cathleen took Caden out in a two-person scull and it didn't take long until they were working well together. The lake was quiet, and the peacefulness nursed his psyche. As they put the scull away, John called to Cathleen. "Gonna miss you girl. And I know the group will too. You're welcome to come back any-time."

They were an hour into the drive north, when Caden, stretched out in the passenger seat, said, "Have you resolved the confusion you were feeling when we talked in January? You've haven't said much."

Cathleen glanced at him. "The same way you haven't said why you broke it off with Quinn."

Caden put his head back and closed his eyes. In a flurry of words, he described the scene in February when he stumbled into the snow. "I don't trust myself." He took a deep breath.

She's the first person I've told other than Jean. But I want her to know she can trust me enough to open up. She needs that and I don't think she's had it.

Several miles passed before Cathleen started talking. "After I got back, I went on a couple of dates." Her glance slid to him again. "With guys. I quickly knew I wasn't attracted to them. I have a friend who's a lesbian. She was one of the first people I met here. A month ago, I told her a capsule version of what happened and that I was curious. She asked me what I wanted." There was a long pause before Cathleen continued. "When do we ever get asked what we want? You know?"

Caden nodded.

"It was easier to tell her what I didn't want. I would be moving back to New England no matter what, so I wasn't looking for a relationship. But I also wasn't interested in a one-night stand. I think I'm the kind of person who needs to be emotionally invested before I start a physical relationship. And I for sure, didn't want a graphic description of what their sex life was like."

Caden chuckled and Cathleen shrugged before laughing along with him.

"Anyway, she and her partner took me to a gay bar. Seeing the women dancing together, and being affectionate with each other, it was a turn on." She sighed. "Reggie came in after we'd been there for a while and that kind of ruined the night for me. But I want to explore that world. I'm going to look for that community when I get settled."

Caden's first instinct had been to tell her that Quinn had a couple of close friends who were lesbians and maybe she'd be a resource. Then he had remembered, as he always did, that Quinn was no longer a part of his life.

"Please don't tell Mom and Dad. Or the rest of the girls."

"It's not my story to tell Cath. You'll know when the time is right. But I'm here, with no judgement if you need a sounding board."

The rest of the drive had passed without further discussion of their private lives. Cathleen had debated the merits of renting or buying in New Hampshire, and Caden had described the mission program he was thinking about joining.

The trip to North Carolina had solidified Caden's plan to spend two months in Honduras. The few days he'd spent away from Boston had been the best he'd had since February. *Not seeing places I went with Quinn, not remembering her here on the terrace or in my bed will let me finally move on. I'll tell the family at dinner on Friday night and everyone else on Saturday.*

Chapter Fifteen

Quinn Goes To Honduras

July

Quinn

QUINN WOKE UP ON the plane to Honduras and looked at her watch. There were two hours left in her flight, the end of a long day that started with a ride on the Dartmouth Coach to Logan Airport for a nine o'clock flight. *I should be flying to Ireland with Caden.*

Being in Boston had been difficult. She hadn't been there since the last time she visited Caden. It was upsetting to be in the same city as he was, but unable to see him. She had fallen asleep as soon as her flight boarded to escape the turmoil swirling in her head and felt better when she woke up.

So much had gone on since that night in late February. Caden breaking things off had stunned her nearly senseless. Forty-five minutes after he walked out, there was a knock on her door. She rushed to open it, positive he had changed his mind and would be on the other side. But instead of Caden, Sam was standing there, telling her Caden had texted him to say she would need a friend because he had ended things with her.

Quinn's knees had buckled as she started sobbing. Sam scooped her up and went to sit on the couch, holding her as the tears flowed. She still wasn't sure how long they had sat there. Eventually, he carried her up to her bedroom and put her under the covers.

He spent the night in her guest room—actually, he spent the entire weekend there, only leaving to buy food, which he cooked and brought to her room to tempt her to eat. He didn't make her get up or talk, just stayed near in case she needed him.

Quinn had finally climbed out of bed on Sunday to take a shower and pull herself together for work the next day. Sam left on Monday morning, telling her to call if she needed him. She let Ashley know what had happened and asked her to keep it between them, not wanting to endure any pitying looks from her colleagues.

That afternoon, Claire was at her town house with Rory. Quinn held Rory and cried for all she wouldn't have with Caden. James came to pick up the baby, and Claire stayed overnight with her. She was there with Rory the next night as well, and Quinn spent much of the night feeling comforted by cradling the baby in her arms.

Sam came back on Friday night, and Quinn realized they were doing the same thing for her that Caden's friends had done for him. They were keeping her from being alone. And she realized Caden had orchestrated the whole thing to take care of her. She wasn't sure if this made her feel better or worse.

Gradually, she'd picked up the pieces of her broken heart and climbed back to where she had been before the conference in November—content with her job, her friends, and her classes. The three months with Caden had been filled with joyous happiness, and she missed that. She missed *him*. She waited every night at ten thirty for calls that didn't come. Her texts, which she was still sending once a week, remained unanswered.

Her degree program finished in May, which left her a little lost. On a whim, she investigated Medical Mission programs. One speaker at the conference in November had mentioned encouraging staff to take part in humanitarian work like Doctors Without Borders, saying they would return to work as better employees with a fresh outlook. The hospital encouraged it as well, and Quinn hoped some time away from New England would allow her finally to get over Caden.

She chose a clinic in Honduras, and now this plane was getting ready to land there and present Quinn with a new challenge.

Hot and humid air enveloped Quinn as she stepped off the plane. Immediately, she saw a man holding a sign with her name, waiting to drive her to the clinic site. He took her bags and led her to a ragtop jeep. They drove for two hours on a dirt road in the middle of a deep, green jungle. She found the scenery exceptionally beautiful and drank it all in.

The clinic was on the grounds of a now-inactive sugar plantation, and they housed the staff in the plantation owner's manse, which fascinated Quinn despite its run-down condition.

A woman around her age was waiting when Quinn stepped out of the jeep. "Hi, I'm Liz. We're going to be roommates." She was shorter than Quinn, with light-brown hair and green eyes. She spoke with a Southern drawl and seemed very chatty, giving Quinn a thorough account of how things ran and what to expect.

Doctors and nurses rotated in and out for shifts of varying lengths, anything from two weeks to two months or longer. The clinic operated Monday through Saturday morning. There were usually three or four doctors and six to ten nurses. The doctors had their own rooms, while the nurses doubled up.

"I'm having a fling with one of the other nurses and hope you won't mind letting me have the room to myself once in a while," Liz confided. "I'll do the same for you."

Quinn chuckled. "I'll find something to do, but I won't need the same accommodation. Where are you from, anyway?"

"Charleston, South Carolina. Did my accent give it away?" When Quinn nodded, she laughed. "Do you have a significant other back home?"

"I don't, but I also don't do casual sex."

"You might change your mind because there are some *hot* nurses and doctors on staff. Most of the medical work happens in an open-air clinic, but every other week, a doctor and nurse pair up to go out to a remote clinic in the mountains. I did one remote, but I prefer the clinic setting." She smiled. "It's not all work. There are activities on Sundays like hikes into the mountains or trips to the beach. There's a rustic swimming pool on the grounds, but it doesn't get a lot of use."

Quinn's interest was piqued. "I like to swim to unwind. I'll probably give that pool a try."

"Tomorrow will start with an introduction of the people who came in this weekend, and then it will be balls-to-the-wall busy for the rest of the day."

Quinn looked at her watch. It was nearly ten o'clock, and she could barely keep her eyes open. Liz led her to their room, and Quinn slept more soundly than she had in months.

Chapter Sixteen

A Familiar Face

Honduras—The First Week

Quinn

BREAKFAST WAS AVAILABLE AT seven and included bacon, eggs, toast, fresh fruit, and strong coffee. It was served on a large porch, and the morning air was fresh and cooler than the night before had been. A woman with an accent Quinn didn't recognize joined them. "G'Day. I'm Mya." She extended her hand to Quinn.

"Quinn Michaels." She grasped Mya's hand. "Are you Australian?"

"Close. I'm a Kiwi, from New Zealand."

"I was hoping to meet people from other countries." The international component was one reason Quinn had landed at this mission. "How long is your stay?"

"I'm just starting my fourth month of six. How about you?"

"I'm only here for a month. I didn't want to be away from my job for any longer than that."

After eating, Quinn and Liz made their way to an open-air pavilion for the introductions. They sat in the back row, and promptly at eight thirty, a tall man dressed in blue scrubs stood to welcome them. Quinn recognized him as Dr. Paul Jones, the director of the program. She had done a Zoom interview with him. There was a man and a woman at the front of the room, and a man with his head in his hands directly behind Dr. Jones. Quinn assumed they were the doctors.

Dr. Jones talked about how things worked in the clinic, which included much of the same information Liz had given her. He introduced the nurses, who had already been there for a week or more, then moved to the three who had arrived over the weekend.

The first two stood when their names were called, and Quinn inwardly groaned. She hated that kind of thing. Finally, she was the only one left, and Dr. Jones said, "Last but not least, we have a newly minted APRN from Hanover, New Hampshire.

Quinn Michaels, please stand up." She rose, and at the sound of her name, the man behind Dr. Jones snapped his head up and looked directly into Quinn's eyes.

"Oh my God," she murmured, thunderstruck. "Caden."

Her heart raced and her face flushed as she sat down. Dr. Jones then introduced the doctors, including, as she already knew, Dr. Caden Brady from Mass General.

As the meeting ended, waves of nausea overtook her, and she scrambled to her feet, hoping to find a place to be sick in private. Liz followed, not saying a word but leading her to a trash can, which they got to just in time before Quinn lost all her breakfast. She attributed it to the travel, the heat, the strong coffee—anything but the real reason.

How the hell am I going to work alongside Caden?

As Liz was showing Quinn the way to the clinic, they bumped into Dr. Jones and two of the other doctors. "Dr. Jones," Quinn said. "It's nice to meet you in person."

"Quinn, it's nice to meet you too. This is Janet Peters and Ian Miller. I'm not sure where Dr. Brady went, but you'll meet him eventually. I trust Liz has given you a thorough introduction to everything. She could run the place."

A blush spread across Liz's cheeks, but Quinn sensed he meant it with respect.

"We'll see you in the clinic," Dr. Jones said as the trio continued walking in the opposite direction.

Liz waved, then turned to Quinn. "Dr. Brady is handsome but kind of standoffish. Not unfriendly, but he doesn't socialize with anyone. Totally keeps to himself."

Quinn wasn't surprised. She knew he'd maintained a distance from the staff at Mass General, too.

They arrived at the clinic, where Quinn worked on intake to give her an introduction to how it functioned. Liz was not exaggerating when she said it would be balls to the wall. There was a steady stream of patients all day, with only a quick break for lunch.

At the end of the day, Liz showed Quinn around more of the grounds before they went back to the manse, where they returned to their room to change before dinner. Quinn had enjoyed having her mind focused on the patients, and the people she met were open and welcoming. Liz was a chatterbox, sure, but friendly and a very capable nurse.

Quinn and Liz ate dinner on the porch with several of the other staff, who told her there was usually a card game going on in the evening and pointed out the fire pit nearby. The porch also boasted several hammocks, which appealed to Quinn as a place to relax and read or journal. She hung out on the porch for a couple of hours, getting to know Mya and Liz better, then went to the pool.

She lowered herself into the water, which was refreshingly cool, and started swimming laps. For the first time since early morning, her mind drifted back to Caden. He had worked as far from her as possible, meaning she barely saw him. Maybe that was how it would be for the entire month.

Claire had continued to stay in touch with her, calling or texting often and showing up to stay with her at random times. Quinn had shared her plans with her. *Claire had to know that Caden was here. She never said a thing.*

However, there were several medical missionary programs in Honduras, so perhaps Claire thought Quinn and Caden would be at different locations. *I've purposely not asked about Caden and Claire has volunteered nothing. I don't think she would have talked about me to him, either.*

Caden

Caden's entire world tilted on its axis when Paul introduced Quinn. She was the last person he expected to see. Paul always did individual introductions in addition to the mass one, so Caden left the pavilion quickly to avoid getting tangled up in that. Quinn worked on intake, so he stationed himself in a back corner of the clinic.

When the clinic closed for the day, relief that he had avoided coming face-to-face with her washed over him.

Caden saw her on the porch after dinner, but didn't think she had seen him. She wore cutoffs with a tank top. He'd never seen her in summer clothes.

Coming to Honduras had been doing exactly what he'd hoped for. The days were hectic, leaving no time to think about anything but the medicine. The need here was so great, the people so poor, that it was giving him a new outlook. He'd been at the clinic for one month, had another month to go and he was becoming more at peace.

He knew Claire had stayed in touch with Quinn, but she had told him nothing about what was going on with her.

Did she know Quinn was coming to Honduras?

He sent Claire a text.

> *Caden: Did you know Quinn was coming here, to the same place where I am, for missionary work?*

> *Claire: No, I knew she was going to Honduras, but I know there are several programs there. Swear to God, I had nothing to do with her being there. Have you talked to her?*

> *Caden: No, she just arrived yesterday. I think she was as shocked to see me as I was to see her.*

> *Claire: Maybe it's a sign—just sayin'...*

Claire had made it clear to him she thought ending things with Quinn was a big mistake, so he knew Claire would think it was a sign. He shook his head, trying to clear his thoughts. It was inevitable they would work together at some point, as the nurses rotated among the doctors. He wanted to see her nursing skills in action, so that excited a small part of him.

One thing he was very sure of—his attraction to her was as strong now as it had been in February. His cock jumped to attention when he heard her name and again at seeing her in the shorts and tank top.

Somehow, the week passed without them coming face-to-face. Caden glimpsed Quinn every night, feeling somewhat like a peeping Tom, and continued to be aroused just at the sight of her.

On Sunday morning, there was a hike taking off at nine, and Caden was trying to decide whether to go. His only socialization had been with the other doctors, but mostly, he kept to himself. Quinn would be on the hike—that was a given. It was killing him being close to her and acting like she didn't exist.

He finally decided he would go on the hike with no expectation of what might happen, just like when he sent her the first text.

Chapter Seventeen
A Hike And A Fall

Honduras—The Second Week

Quinn

QUINN KNEW SHE AND Caden would meet at some point, and she was nervous about it, but other than that, she loved her time at the clinic. The days were very busy with a variety of cases. Every evening, she spent time on the porch, sometimes playing cards and other times reading in a hammock. She and Liz were becoming firm friends, and she knew it was a friendship that would last even after they went home. Her nights ended at the pool, swimming laps.

On Saturday night, Liz was busy with Marc, the nurse she had mentioned to Quinn the first night, so Quinn relaxed by the fire pit near the porch. She added more wood to the small fire that was already burning, then stretched out in one of the lounge chairs. Sipping her glass of wine and gazing into the flames, she thought of home. She couldn't believe a week had gone by already. *It would be perfect if Caden wasn't here. I told Sam I was coming here to clear my head, and it's hard to stop thinking about Cade when I see him every day.*

Mya appeared, carrying a bottle of wine, interrupting Quinn's thoughts. "Mind if I join you?"

"Oh, please do." Quinn loved Mya's accent and welcomed the chance to get to know her better. "I haven't met anyone staying as long as you are. How'd that come about?"

"It's unusual for certain." Mya took a swallow of her wine. "I wasn't ready to return to New Zealand. Paul knew and offered this as a refuge."

Mya's language intrigued Quinn. *Maybe I'm not the only one escaping the past.* "A refuge?"

"I sound very melodramatic, don't I? I'd been in the United States for a couple of years working as a traveling nurse. I was ready to leave but not ready to return to my parents' house."

"How old are you?" Quinn was certain Mya was younger than she was.

"Twenty-five. I worked for a year after I finished university, but then I just needed to get away. My parents were acting like I was still thirteen." She took another long swallow. "I've made enough money to move into my own place once I know where I want to be. I'm still trying to figure that out."

"Where were you in the US?"

"On the west coast. Northern California, a short while in Oregon, and then almost a year in Seattle. I met Paul in Cali. He left there to come here, and we stayed in touch."

"I lived in Seattle for a bit." Quinn named the hospital where she'd worked, and Mya wasn't familiar with it. "Did you ever eat at Bella Bocca?" Quinn asked, naming her favorite Italian restaurant.

"Yes! I loved it there. Was Mauricio tending bar?"

"He was! I can't believe he hasn't moved on. He was such a sweetheart." Quinn smiled. She felt like she was talking to an old friend as the two of them discovered more places they had both enjoyed.

The fire had burned out, and Quinn pulled a hoodie over her head. "Are you going on the hike tomorrow?"

"Yes. I love hiking."

On Sunday morning, while waiting for the hike to start, Quinn talked with Mya about trails near Seattle. Liz and Marc joined them, and shortly after, Caden walked up to the group. Dr. Jones greeted him and said how happy he was to have Caden joining them.

Liz did a double take at the sight of Caden. "Wow, he's done nothing with us before. Wonder what's up?"

Quinn suspected *she* was what was up, but she would not share that with her new friends. She had felt his eyes on her every night, but he had not sought her out, and the first move was not going to come from her.

They started up the mountain path with Mya at Paul's side. Quinn walked alongside Liz and Caden was behind them. She could hear him talking with Dr. Miller and remembered Christmas Eve when he admitted the first thing he noticed about her was her butt. She wondered if he was enjoying the view. Quinn's heart was pounding, and she knew it wasn't just because of the uphill climb.

At the summit, they found a spectacular vista of the neighboring mountains. There were several paths to explore, but before they did, Dr. Jones gathered them all for a photo. Quinn hung out with Liz and Marc for a little while, but figuring they might like some time alone, she wandered off by herself.

The spot where Dr. Jones had taken the picture was very scenic, and she snapped some pictures of the view before starting down another trail. She stopped at an overlook to take more pictures and sensed someone behind her. She turned to see Caden.

Her stomach knotted, but nothing like the first day. *I knew this time would come. I can do this. I can talk to him like I talk to everyone else here.*

"Is that picture going on your gallery wall?" His voice was hoarse.

Quinn kept hers light. "I hope so."

"Am I still in the gallery?"

She looked at him, even more handsome with a slight tan, wearing the same Red Sox cap and sneakers he had in December. "Yes." And tears sprang into her eyes. *Damn it all!* She hurriedly wiped them away.

"You finished your program, an advanced-practice registered nurse. I'm proud of you."

"Yeah, it was an easier semester." She paused. "Well, that's not exactly true. The courses were easier, but everything else was harder, a lot fucking harder. But yes, I finished. You must be done as well?"

"No, I took a leave."

She frowned. "That's surprising."

He took a step toward her. "Quinn, I'm so sor..."

Before he could finish, Liz and Marc came around the corner, laughing. They stopped, and Liz said, "Dr. Brady, it was nice of you to join us."

"Liz, we've been working together for a month. You can call me Caden."

"Okay, Caden." Liz smiled. "Did you enjoy the hike?"

"I did, although I'd be enjoying this moment a little more if Nurse Michaels wasn't standing right on the edge of that ledge."

Quinn stepped back onto the trail. *So, I'm Nurse Michaels, but Liz gets invited to use his first name. He's working overtime to hide the fact that we know each other.*

"So sorry for scaring you, Dr. Brady." She was burning to know why he had taken a leave from his courses.

The rest of the hikers rejoined them, and they started down the mountain, with Caden and Dr. Miller taking the lead alongside Paul. Quinn noticed Caden stayed as far from the edge of the path as possible. Mya walked by her side and they chatted about more mountains they had climbed on the west coast.

Caden

Caden tried to pay attention to the conversation between Paul and Dr. Miller, but all he could think about was Quinn. He'd seen the tears that filled her eyes when he asked about the picture of them from their first weekend together. *It's been four months, and she hasn't taken it down. She needs to. I don't want her pining for me.* He was deep in his thoughts when he heard a noise behind him.

"Whoa." Mya stumbled as she turned her ankle on the rocky path.

Caden turned around just as she careened off the trail and down the side of the mountain. Terror washed over him as Mya screamed while desperately trying to grab branches, boulders, anything to stop her fall. The group was stunned into silence as they watched her plummet.

When Mya finally stopped tumbling, chaos broke out as everyone started talking at once. Before they formulated a plan to reach her, Quinn stepped off the path and started picking her way down to Mya, who had gone completely still.

The terror that had Caden in its grasp increased tenfold. "Quinn! What the fuck! Quinn, stop." The alarm in his voice was apparent and he could feel the eyes boring into him. He took a step toward the edge, then backed away. "Quinn, you need to stop. Come back."

Paul placed his hand on Caden's arm. "What's going on?"

"It's dangerous. She's going to get hurt."

"She seems to know what she's doing." Paul's eyes were on Caden for several seconds before he turned back to the group. "We'll let Quinn get to Mya so we can figure out what is needed.

The group stood quietly, watching Quinn's careful footfalls. She paused, seeming to assess the best way forward, then continued until her foot slid on loose gravel and she slipped several feet before she steadied herself.

Caden gasped as she skidded on the rocks and saw Paul give him the same look as earlier. *I should say something. Give him some kind of explanation, but I can't.* Quinn finally reached Mya, and Caden let go of the tension he'd been feeling.

The air was perfectly quiet, and the doctors and nurses gathered above could hear every word Quinn said. "Mya, it's me Quinn." She kneeled by her side and grasped her arm. "Can you open your eyes?" Quinn looked up and called, more loudly, "She's alive." There was a pause and then, "Oh thank God, she's opening her eyes." She turned back to Mya. "Don't move. Where does it hurt?"

"Everywhere," Mya groaned.

"We're going to need help down here." Quinn was looking up the hill again. "I'm not sure how badly she's hurt. I don't want to move her, and I don't think she'll be able to climb back up."

There was a brief discussion before Paul took charge. "We will not risk anyone else being hurt and we don't all need to be down there. I'm going, and Cade, I'd like you with me because you have the most emergency experience. I have very basic first aid supplies in my backpack." He looked around. "A couple of you should start back. Keep trying your phones until you have service. Call the clinic, tell them what has happened. They should drive as far as they can to meet us. Ask them to improvise a way to transport Mya down this path to the road. The rest of you stay here until we figure out what we are dealing with." With that, he stepped off the path much as Quinn had done and signaled for Caden to follow him. "Let's go."

Caden stood at the edge of the path, watching Paul navigate the steep slope for a few seconds. The drop into nothingness made his head spin, and he closed his eyes to make it stop. Opening them, he ran his hand through his hair. *This is my worst nightmare.* He stepped a tentative toe into the void, took a deep breath, and followed Paul's lead.

Paul kept up constant chatter as they descended. "I'm the one who encouraged her to come here. She wanted to experience something other than the big city hospitals she worked at in the States. She became like a daughter to me when we worked together in California. I'll never forgive myself if something happens to her."

The words washed over Caden as he concentrated on the steep descent in front of him, carefully placing each step and breathing deeply. *I don't know where the fuck this damn phobia came from, but it's time to get over it.* During the brief moments he lifted his eyes away from the ground, he looked toward Quinn, still kneeling next to Mya. The sound of his breathing blocked out the words she was saying to Mya, but he could hear the comfort in her tone. Concentrating on that eased his distress, and he began to relax and caught up to Paul shortly before they reached Quinn and Mya.

Paul immediately dropped to his knees, taking Mya's hand. "What are you going to do for your next trick, my little bird?"

She responded with a weak smile and a shrug. "Not sure."

"Caden's an emergency department doc. He's going to look you over." Paul looked up at him and nodded for him to get started.

Quinn moved aside, giving Caden room to work. "Hey, that was quite a tumble. Any spot hurt more than others?"

"My left shoulder and my ribs. I'm sure they're cracked."

Caden manipulated her shoulder, and she cried out in pain. He frowned. "Sorry. At the least you've dislocated your shoulder, more likely, you've broken your collarbone. How's your breathing?"

"Hurts to take a deep breath."

Caden nodded as he gently turned her neck. "Did you lose consciousness?" When Mya shrugged, he looked at Quinn.

"She was unconscious when I got here but came to right after. I'm not sure how long it took me."

Caden caught her eye. "Too long." Quinn's eyes opened wide, and he realized how she had interpreted his words. "It was hell watching you climb down that mountain." He returned his attention to Mya. "We'll figure you have a concussion, hopefully minor."

After checking her other arm, he moved down to her legs. Mya winced in pain when he touched her left ankle. Caden looked at Paul. "There's no way she's walking out of here."

Paul nodded. "Let's get her sitting up. See how that goes."

Mya tolerated that and a cheer went up from the crowd above. She took a couple of deep breaths. "My head hurts, and I'm dizzy." She retched, turning her head to the side.

Caden looked across her at Paul and said softly, "Definitely a concussion. We need to get her out of here as quickly as possible." He stood while Paul continued to support Mya. Looking first at the steep embankment they had just climbed down and then to his right, he turned to Quinn. "What if we walk that way instead of going back up? We'll intersect with the path eventually and we'll be that much closer to the road." When she didn't immediately respond, he said, "Am I reading that right?"

She studied the landscape, finally agreeing. "You are. That should get us out of here the quickest."

Caden said, "Let's get going." Looking at Paul, he added, "Do you know how to do chair carry?"

Paul huffed. "I was a Boy Scout, earned my first aid badge." He called to the group waiting at the top, telling them to start back.

After the men lifted her, Quinn positioned Mya's arms, then picked up Paul's backpack and led the way, watching for hazards. By the time they reached the path, both men were dripping with sweat. The rest of the group was waiting and Ian said, "The jeep's waiting right around the corner. Marc and I can take her if you want a break."

Paul glanced at Caden, who shook his head. "No, we're good. Is an ambulance on the way? We need to get her to the hospital."

"I called. They'll rendezvous with the jeep."

They had Mya loaded into the jeep within minutes. Paul climbed into the backseat beside her, then looked back. "Caden, come with us. Quinn, your help was invaluable today."

Caden stopped before climbing in, and his eyes drilled into Quinn. "We'll call and let you know how she is."

Chapter Eighteen
An Uneasy Reunion

Quinn

BACK AT THE MANSE, the only thing Quinn wanted to do was flop onto her bed, but Marc convinced her to join everyone on the porch. "You were such a badass, charging into action. We need to drink to that."

Quinn had finished one glass of wine when Paul called Ian to say he and Caden were on the way home. Mya was scratched and bruised, but her only serious injuries were a broken collarbone and a concussion. They were keeping her in the hospital for a couple of days, and she was adamant that she was going to return to the clinic. Marc handed Quinn a second glass of wine and, after a couple of sips, she felt the tension ebbing out of her body. Paul's call put everyone in a good mood, and she watched them laughing and joking for a few minutes before she stood.

"I'm going to swim some laps. I'll see you all tomorrow." The cool water washed away the rest of her stress and, after several laps, Quinn flipped onto her back. Caden's screams, after she had started down the mountainside, pounded in her head. He'd been so unfeeling in front of Liz and Marc. *I can't believe he reacted like that. Does it mean he still cares as much as I do?*

Quinn was nearly asleep when Liz returned to their room, screeching as she walked in the door. "What was that all about with Dr. Brady?"

"What?" Quinn mumbled.

"The way he reacted when you took off down that mountain. It was over the top."

She'd been expecting this and had an answer ready. "He must have a thing about heights. You saw how he said he didn't like me standing on that ledge. It must have freaked him out, seeing Mya fall and then me following her." She burrowed under the covers. "I need to go to sleep. Between the hike, the adrenaline rush and that wine, I'm exhausted."

"I think he likes you." Liz enjoyed getting the last word.

The next morning, Quinn worked with Caden. She'd known it would happen and was glad they broke the ice the day before—it took some of the sting out, even if he acted like he'd just met her. They dove right into treating patients without even a word about what happened the day before. It surprised her to hear him speaking Spanish to the patients. *Is that an example of how very little I really knew about him?*

Shortly before noon, a teenager came in with a nasty laceration on his leg. It was going to need stitches, so Quinn gathered the supplies and assisted Caden. The prior week had been filled with inoculations, sore throats, and ear flushes. She was happy to be doing something meatier.

When they finished, Caden turned away from her, then turned back and asked, "Do you want to walk up to lunch?"

Quinn hesitated. "With you?"

"Yeah, it looks like there's a bit of a breather."

Quinn shrugged her shoulders in response, unable to form words. *Get a grip on yourself!* They walked in silence, filled their plates, and sat together on the porch.

"You're an excellent nurse." Caden kept his eyes on his plate. "I figured you were, but it's nice to see you in action."

"Thanks. It's nice seeing you doctoring too. You speak Spanish. That surprised me."

"I'm hardly fluent, but I try. I took it in high school and picked up some in the ED."

"Well, you are far ahead of me, and the patients seem to appreciate it."

A long silence followed before Caden spoke again. This time, he looked Quinn in the eyes. "You were amazing yesterday. The way you went to Mya."

"I knew what I was doing."

Caden nodded.

They had almost finished eating when Liz walked by. She smirked at Quinn, and Quinn smiled back, knowing what Liz was thinking. Liz's eyebrows shot up, and Quinn shook her head. The exchange between them was impossible to miss, so of course, Caden asked what was going on.

"Apparently, you're a hot commodity here, and Liz thinks I should go after you."

He huffed out an amused breath. "Are you going to?"

"No, I didn't come here with that in mind, and I don't do casual sex." She looked pointedly at him.

He frowned. "What did you come for?"

"I was at loose ends when school finished, and I needed to reset my mind. How about you?"

"I'd gone through a rough few months and needed to get out of my head. This has been good." He looked out from the porch. "It's so busy I don't have time to dwell on my issues, and when I see the poverty, I realize how fortunate I am."

Her heart jumped at his mention of a "rough few months." He was saying so much in just a few words. "Yeah, I've only been here a week, but I already feel like I'll go back to Dartmouth with a better outlook."

Midafternoon, a preteen girl came in with severe stomach pains. As Caden was examining her, she began to retch. Quinn grabbed an emesis bag and held it to her mouth. The girl emptied her stomach into the bag, and Caden held her hair out of the way as she was vomiting.

Quinn watched him over the girl's head and remembered him holding her hair when she was sick after the New Year's Eve party.

When the vomiting stopped, Caden continued his exam and asked Quinn to draw blood to check the girl's white blood count. His diagnosis was an appendix about to burst. There was a sterile area in the clinic where they could perform surgery in an emergency, so they moved her there.

"Paul," Caden called to Dr. Jones. "I've got a hot appendix. I think the surgery needs to be done now rather than risk the two-hour drive to the city."

Dr. Jones examined the girl. "I agree. Quinn, you can assist."

"I'm not a surgical nurse. There must be someone else."

"None of the nurses on staff are surgical. You'll be fine."

Caden spoke then, soothingly. "I'll tell you exactly what I need."

Caden turned out to be right. The appendix was on the verge of rupturing, and the girl never would have made it to the city hospital. The surgery took just over an hour and exhilarated Quinn. She relished watching Caden work and felt proud of her role.

They were going to keep the girl in the sterile unit until at least the next day. Her mother would stay with her, but a nurse needed to be there as well. Quinn and Liz volunteered, with Quinn staying until midnight and Liz relieving her until morning.

Caden returned around eleven to check on the patient and asked Quinn to come outside to talk. He gave her instructions, then added, "You did an excellent job today. You have a calm demeanor, and you anticipated what I needed even though you have limited surgical experience."

She smiled. "Thank you. It was an outstanding experience. I did a surgical rotation, but it was years ago, and I didn't have half the knowledge I have now." She paused and met his gaze. "Your praise means a lot to me."

Caden

Quinn and Caden worked together the next day, and Paul asked Caden to stop by his office after dinner. Caden joined a large group for dinner, including Quinn, then went to see Paul.

"You and Quinn work well together." Paul's words were both a declaration and a question.

Caden nodded. "I like her quiet disposition, and she doesn't seem prone to dramatics."

"I want to send the two of you into the mountains to run the remote clinic this week."

They did the remote clinics every other week, and Caden had done one during his first month, accompanied by Marc.

Caden hesitated, not sure what it would be like being with Quinn for almost forty-eight hours straight—and with no idea how she would feel about it. "You should consult Quinn before making a final decision."

Paul tilted his head questioningly toward Caden. "Something going on? You've been different since she arrived—going on the hike, eating lunch with her yesterday, to say nothing of your reaction when she took off after Mya. I don't have a problem with it. My job doesn't include policing the staff's love life. Just wondering."

Caden hesitated again. "We know each other." Paul remained quiet, letting Caden elaborate. "We met last November at a conference. We dated."

"Past tense? You seem to get along well."

Caden took a deep breath, blew it out, and then did it again. "It was serious, but I broke it off in February because I had some issues I needed to deal with. Seeing her has shown me my feelings haven't changed. Not sure how she feels. Our only interactions have been professional."

Paul nodded. "I'll talk to her because I talk to all the staff before I send them remote. They need to know it could be dangerous and the living conditions are unsophisticated. But to reference my earlier comment, I'm not getting involved in your love life."

After a pause, Paul added with a smile, "She swims every night at nine thirty if you want to see her in a nonprofessional setting."

Shortly after nine thirty, Caden started down the path to the pool. His heart was racing, and his palms were sweaty, but he needed to talk to Quinn before they went up into the mountains.

Quinn was already in the pool, and as Caden watched her arms slicing through the water, he remembered the grace and form he'd seen when they went skiing. He settled on one of the ancient loungers and admired her as she effortlessly went from one end of the pool to the other.

When she finished, Quinn climbed out at the opposite end of the pool from Caden, and he watched as she toweled off. She started down the path to the manse, still towel drying her hair as she walked. Not wanting to frighten her, he softly called, "Quinn."

Her head snapped up, and she dropped the towel over her shoulders. "Caden, you startled me! What are you doing here?"

He stood. "Did Paul talk to you about doing the remote clinic?"

She straightened. "Yes, and I told him I'd be happy to do it."

"With me?"

"Yes, with you. I know you'll keep me safe if the need arises."

Caden's heartbeat had returned to normal while he watched her swimming, but at her words, it started to hammer again. *Even after what I did, she trusts me.* "Were you as surprised to see me here as I was to see you?"

"Oh, hell yes! I lost my breakfast... and I hadn't even had anything to drink." She laughed a little. "But it hasn't been as bad as I imagined."

Caden wasn't sure he agreed. His emotions had kept him tied in knots since that first morning. *It's because I'm the one who walked away, and I'm wracked with guilt because I hurt her.*

"Why did you take a leave from your degree program? I wanted to ask you Sunday, but not in front of Liz."

"Mmm," he said. "Had to act like we don't know each other."

She frowned. "You weren't leaping in there to admit you knew me, calling me 'Nurse Michaels.'"

"I didn't know what to do, Quinn. I wasn't sure if you'd even talk to me."

She blinked, and he realized she was tearing up. "I didn't know what to do either. That's why I was vomiting into a trash can that first morning. You didn't answer my question—why'd you take a leave?"

He swallowed. "Because I needed to work on myself. I started going to therapy twice a week. That seemed more important than advancing my career. A career that means nothing if my personal life is a mess."

"Has it helped?"

"I've developed some coping techniques, like deep breathing. Although honestly, I've had that one since December. I used it when we ran into Sam on our ski weekend. It worked there, and I was foolish enough to think it would always work." He put his hand on his chest. "But that morning…" He looked at Quinn, knowing despair showed in his eyes. "That morning in February, I couldn't even catch my breath."

Quinn's eyes filled with tears again.

"I've been journaling." He paused and sighed. "Ironic, since that's how I found out about Mary. And I even joined a support group."

"A support group?"

"Yeah, a support group for men who have suffered trauma."

Unbelievably, she giggled. "I'm sorry. I can't see you talking in a group."

He chuckled. "I know. I wouldn't have pictured it either. But my therapist recommended it. And it's given me some different perspectives. I've heard some horrific stories." He rubbed his jaw. "You're in better shape than I am. You followed your plan, and you're embracing this experience, meeting new people, while I've been isolating myself. I'm sure your roommate told you I haven't taken part in any of the social stuff here."

She snorted. "Liz mentioned something about the hot but standoffish doctor." Her expression changed. "It hasn't been easy. I've missed you so much."

"I am so sorry for the pain I caused you." Caden reached for her.

"No, don't touch me."

It was a valid request. He stepped back and looked away, quiet for a minute. "I adopted a kitten." He fished his phone out of his pocket. "Want to see a picture?"

She clapped her hands and beamed. "Yes, please!"

Quinn studied the picture of a tiny, gray kitten. "So small! Male or female?"

"A girl. The fifteen-year-old boy in me decided I needed her. She... she fills an empty spot."

"What's her name?"

He looked directly into her eyes as he answered. "Aurora."

Quinn blinked. "That's..." She stopped and cleared her throat. "That's..." She looked at the ground.

Caden made sure that when she lifted her head, he looked into her eyes.

She finally found her voice. "Who's taking care of her while you're here?"

"She's with my parents. How about Max?"

A smile crossed her face. "Same. A sad substitute for grand-children."

Caden nodded. "I'm sure that's how my mother feels." He finally looked away. "I've missed you too. I fought with myself every single day, wanting to text you, to call you—hell, to drive to Hanover. And it's not only wanting to make love to you.

Something happens every day, and I wonder what you'd think or say if I told you." He paused. "Where do we go from here?"

"It was your idea to leave. Are you saying you want me back? Because I can't go through losing you again. You walking out that door gutted me. Do you think the PTRS is gone, cured, whatever?"

"I honestly don't know, and I don't want to start something and risk hurting you again. But friends? Can we at least be friends? And acknowledge we know each other? I gave Dr. Jones a capsule version of our history."

"Colleagues," Quinn whispered. "Let's start with colleagues and see what happens."

Quinn

Quinn slowly walked back to the manse. When Caden had stepped out of the shadows at the pool, her stomach quivered the same way it had when they talked on the phone before their first date. And when he told her the name of his kitten, memories of that first date had cascaded over her.

As soon as she entered their room, Liz pounced on Quinn. "You're never this late. It worried me, so I walked down to the pool. You were there talking to Dr. Brady, and it looked intense. What's going on?" Liz was being uncharacteristically serious. "I know I talk a lot, but I don't gossip. Think about it—I haven't told you anything about who's doing who. You can talk to me, and it won't go anywhere."

Quinn appreciated her concern. "Oh man, it's a long story. I met Caden last November at a conference in Boston. We started dating, and it was good, fantastic, in fact. Neither of us was looking for casual sex. We took it slow, and we fell in love." She paused, taking a deep breath. "We're probably still in love. But he had some issues from a former relationship, and at the end of February, he broke up with me. That first morning when I was sick. It was from the shock of seeing him here."

Liz's mouth hung open. "Why end it if he's still in love with you?"

"This needs to stay between us." She told Liz how he'd found Mary in bed with someone and started having panic attacks after getting involved with Quinn. "He had one last winter that was so severe he went outside to get a grip on himself. He was barefoot." She looked at Liz. "You understand—there's snow on the ground in February. He broke up with me the next weekend."

"Damn, Quinn, that's messed up." Liz shook her head. "And I can't picture calm and in-control Dr. Brady losing it like that."

"Neither could I. It devastated me. We were great together. It's been several months, and I'm still not over it. After talking to him, I don't think he is either. He's been working to get his mental health straightened out. Said he's been seeing a therapist twice a week."

Liz nodded. "So, what now?"

"We're going to acknowledge we know each other. But I will not jump back in only to have it implode again. I don't know how he's going to know he's 'better' or 'cured.' And we're going to do the remote clinic on Thursday and Friday."

Liz scoffed. "You don't need to worry about getting swept away in the heat of a moment up there. It's the least romantic place I've ever been."

"That's good to know, but I'm not worried about it. I don't think either of us is looking for that right now."

"Okay." Liz hesitated. "But you have to tell me—was it as hot as I've dreamed about with someone who looks like he does?"

Quinn sighed. "It was even better than you could imagine. But maybe that's because there was a lot of feeling behind it. We were exceptionally close, in all ways."

Liz gave her a hug and told her she hoped everything would work out.

Chapter Nineteen

Quinn and Caden Go Remote

Quinn

AFTER THE CLINIC CLOSED on Wednesday afternoon, Caden and Quinn loaded the jeep with the supplies they would need.

"Bedrolls?" Quinn asked. *What have I gotten myself into?*

"There are cots in the cabin. We make them up when we get there and strip them before we leave. It's rustic. Paul told you, didn't he?"

"Um, yeah, but maybe I wasn't paying enough attention. It'll be okay, right? I can do anything for one night." She was talking more to herself than to Caden.

Caden chuckled. "It'll be an experience. It's not the Back Bay."

Getting to the remote site meant a long drive on a narrow mountain road. There were spots with deep ravines on either side, and Quinn watched Caden as he stared straight ahead, taking deep breaths and gripping the side of the jeep. Paired with his reactions on Sunday, Quinn knew she was seeing the real evidence of his height phobia here in Honduras.

A volley of gunshots echoed over the mountains from far away, and Quinn jumped at the sound. Still looking straight ahead, Caden put his hand over hers. She knew he was trying to reassure her and didn't shy away. It was a comfort to feel his warmth.

There were already patients waiting when they arrived at the cabin, and they spent the day doing vaccinations, dispensing antibiotics, and doing follow-ups on the patients from two weeks earlier. The stream of patients finally let up around six, and Quinn asked, "Where did they all come from? And how do they know we are here?" Caden told her they lived in the mountains and word of mouth let them know about the clinic.

The cabin had no electricity or running water, just kerosene lights and a gas refrigerator and stove. There were four cots, and the bathroom had a composting toilet. Quinn understood why

Liz said it wasn't romantic and why she didn't want to come back.

Quinn made her bed and checked to see what they had for food. They had picked up a cooler from the kitchen before they left, and it had their food for the evening and the next day, as well as utensils and plates. She realized, with some sadness, there would not be coffee in the morning.

Quinn told Caden she had never used a gas stove, and he took over cooking steak for the two of them plus the driver and bodyguard. Caden set a couple of blankets on a grassy area and told her, "Think of it as a picnic."

The one positive she could find was that the cooler had beer in it. "You are enjoying this far more than a city boy from Boston ought to. This isn't even rural New Hampshire."

Caden laughed and told her he found it a refreshing change.

They finished eating, and Caden gathered everything to take back the next day. "Look at it this way. At least there aren't any dishes to wash." He was more relaxed than she had seen him since she'd arrived. He handed her another beer and told her they had to stay out until dark to see the stars.

Quinn drank part of the beer and lay back on the blanket. It was completely quiet. The driver and bodyguard had gone into the cabin, and she tried to absorb the peace of the moment. Having Caden so close was a distraction, and her thoughts were full of the memory of his hands on her body and his lips on hers. She concentrated on her breathing to clear her mind before sitting up to drink the rest of her beer.

Caden watched her. "Hey, you never told me exactly how much alcohol leads to you being sick. You do not want to get to that point up here."

She snorted. "I'm never going to live that down, am I? I'm good for two or three beers. You should probably shut me off." Then she realized it had gone dark, and there was a faint crescent moon in a sky filled with stars. "Those stars are incredible."

"They blew my mind my very first night at the clinic. And then I came up here, and they are even brighter. You don't see the stars like this in Boston. And the quiet is amazing. This has been very healing for me."

A combination of sad and happy tears sprang to her eyes. Sad for the pain he'd been in, and happy he seemed to have found peace. Quinn realized no matter what happened, she wanted Caden to be happy and whole.

Maybe that was genuine love, wanting happiness for the person you care for, even if they weren't with you.

She didn't trust herself to say anything, so she just gazed at the night sky.

After a while, Caden stood, reaching down to help her to her feet. "We should go to bed. We'll need to be ready early, and it'll be a full day."

His hand on hers as he pulled her up was like a lightning strike to her heart. Wondering if he felt the same thing but afraid to ask, she said the first thing that came into her mind. "And with no coffee."

In the morning, they stripped their beds, ate some fruit, and prepared to take on the patients. Quinn had never felt less prepared to face a day. The patients started coming at eight.

Midafternoon, the sound of gunfire shattered the air. Quinn jumped. "What the fuck was that?"

Caden spoke to the bodyguard in Spanish and relayed the conversation to her. "Probably drug runners. He doesn't think they'll come any closer."

"Damn, I don't like that." Her heart felt like it would beat out of her chest.

Caden put his hand over hers. "We'll be okay."

Quinn was relieved to start the drive back to the clinic, and she was more comfortable talking to Caden than she had been on the drive the day before. "So, you've gone from seeing your therapist twice a week to nothing since you've been here?"

"Nope, I talk to her on the phone on Tuesday and Thursday. Obviously, I missed last night."

"Did you tell her I'm here?" She paused. "Or do I even get talked about? Am I overrating my importance?"

"No, you're not overrating. You get talked about."

She knew therapy was private, so she didn't pursue that. Caden would share if or when he was ready. "It shocked me when you broke things off, but I was equally shocked to open my door and find Sam." She shook her head. "I can't believe you contacted him."

"I didn't want you to be alone, and I knew he was close. It was going to be Sam or Ashley, but I wasn't sure how you'd feel about me contacting a work friend. Claire was my second choice, but that would have gotten messy." He sighed. "Actually, I called Claire the next day, and it *did* get messy. She was pissed at me in the way only an older sister can be. Truth be told, she's still pissed at me."

But Quinn couldn't let go of the mystery of Sam. "You break up with me because the thought of me with another man drives you over the edge. Then you call the one guy I told you wanted to be with me to let him know I was alone, basically urging him to go to me. It makes no sense."

"Nope, it doesn't." His grin was rueful, and he shrugged. "I've done a lot of things that make little sense. I have no explanation other than I wanted to take care of you somehow."

"Were you concerned I'd sleep with him?"

"Not really. I was pretty sure you wouldn't, and I didn't think he'd try to take advantage of the pain you were in. Turns out I made the right decision."

"How do you know that?"

"Sam's been in touch with me." He smiled. "I've learned he's a nice guy. I sensed he was the one guy in your past who was decent, and I was right."

"Not sure how I feel about that. The idea of you being… what, friends, with my ex-boyfriend?"

"It's not as creepy as it sounds. I told him you could let him know what happened between us, and apparently you did, because he started checking in to see how *I* was doing. He let me know how you were the first time he messaged me, but not much after that. So, what started as a way to help you became something that has helped me."

"I'm not sure I understand."

"Sam gives me a different perspective, like the support group. My entire circle of friends is from high school or college. We've all lived the same life. Sam's life differs from mine, so it widens my viewpoint. You pointed out I'd lived my entire life in Boston. It makes for a narrow focus. You've lived in other places, so you have a wider focus. That's a good thing. And it's something I'm trying to cultivate."

She nodded. "Hence a two-month missionary trip to Honduras."

"Exactly."

Sam had stayed in close contact with Quinn since the night he'd held her while she sobbed. They texted regularly, and he came over for dinner once a month. But she had no idea he was in contact with Caden.

A thought struck her. "Did he know you were coming to Honduras?"

"Yes. We ran into each other at a Red Sox game in May, and I told him."

Quinn just nodded. They were almost back to the manse, and she needed to digest what Caden had told her.

Sam never told me anything. *That sneak. Just wait until I get home.*

Then her thoughts changed. *Caden and I are talking as easily as we did from the first day in Cambridge. The biggest difference is there's none of the intimacy we used to have.* She remembered those phone calls on nights they were apart, when Caden's voice would roll over her like a warm caress. *I miss that so much. It sounds like he's worked hard in therapy.*

Is there any chance for us?

Liz and Marc were watching for them to return and hurried to meet them. "We'll unpack the jeep," Liz said. "Go take a shower. I know how much I wanted one after being in that godforsaken place." Quinn and Caden both protested they could do it, but Liz would not have it. "One of the new nurses brought his guitar. There's going to be music tonight. Go shower, get some food, and join us. Mya came back this morning, so she'll be there too."

Quinn walked up to her room, wondering if Caden would join them as well. She showered, dressed, and went to the kitchen located off the porch where they ate. Starving, she was looking through the fridge when Caden came in.

"Did her invitation include me?"

"I'm sure it did." Quinn hesitated. "Liz saw us talking Tuesday night and wanted to know what was going on. I told her we had dated."

"And I broke your heart."

"Something like that." Her mouth curled up into a sad smile.

They found some food and went out to sit with Liz and Marc. Caden pulled a chair out for Quinn, and all the times he had helped her with her coat or opened the car door came rushing back. Before she sat down, Quinn gently hugged Mya, who had her arm in a sling. "I'm so happy to see you."

"I'm happy to be here. The whole incident, after I twisted my ankle, is a blur, but please know how grateful I am for what you did." Mya's bruises were obvious, but she was in good spirits. "I've convinced Paul to let me stay. There must be something I can do until my collarbone heals."

When they finished eating, Caden gathered their plates and took them to the kitchen. Mya and Liz raised their eyebrows, and Quinn shrugged.

"His manners are amazing." Liz nudged Marc. "You could take lessons."

Marc narrowed his eyes at Caden when he came back. "You are setting the bar way too high, man."

Caden chuckled. "We know how to be gentlemen in Boston. Unlike you heathens from New Jersey." They had already sparred over whether the Yankees or the Red Sox were the better baseball team.

The music was enjoyable, and the five of them chatted about the remote clinic, with Liz and Quinn in agreement about how awful it was and Caden trying to convince them of how valuable it was as a break from civilization. Liz looked at Mya. "You're probably going to miss it altogether. Consider yourself lucky."

Quinn thought about that moment in the mountains when their hands touched and wondered again if Caden had felt the same spark she had. She ached to be close to him again. *This is probably a bad idea.* Her hand reached under the table and slid onto his thigh, and her heart warmed when he flashed a small grin in her direction. She remembered how reassuring his touch had been after the gunfire in the mountains.

Caden continued talking to Marc and Liz as he slowly snaked one hand under the table and found Quinn's. Neither of them moved their hands for the rest of the evening.

Liz told them there was a trip to the beach scheduled for Sunday and asked if they would go. Quinn exclaimed she would, and Caden agreed it sounded like fun.

As the night wound down, Caden said, "Liz, Marc, thanks for unloading the jeep. This was a nice evening. See you all in the morning." He headed toward his room without looking back at Quinn.

Liz hardly let the door to their room close before she said, "My God, the heat between the two of you is palpable!"

Quinn shook her head. "You're imagining things. We didn't even touch each other while you and Marc were sitting there playing kissy-face."

"Didn't even touch!" Liz scoffed. "Don't give me that! I know your hand was on his leg. I'll bet he's taking a cold shower right now."

Quinn laughed. "You're crazy." But she knew the attraction between her and Caden was obvious.

Before she walked away from the table, Mya had grinned and wagged her finger between Caden and Quinn. Then she whispered in her ear. "You owe me an explanation, but wait until this concussion heals. I don't think my brain can take that much stimulation right now."

On Saturday night, the guitar player performed again, and he supplemented it with music from his phone. A couple of people started dancing, and nearly everyone joined them. Dr. Miller came over to Quinn's table and took her hand. "Dance with me."

She joined him, afraid to look back at Caden. Ian presented no threat, as he was very vocal about his love for his wife and how much he missed her, but Quinn knew there was nothing rational about Caden's panic attacks.

The song ended, and she returned to the table. Quietly, Caden asked, "Will you dance with me?"

She nodded, and he took her hand to lead her to the center of the porch. He continued to hold her hand while they danced.

"Are you okay?"

He nodded, looking surprised. "I am."

Later, Marc danced with Quinn while Liz dragged Caden back to the dance floor.

As the evening grew late, Liz whispered in Quinn's ear, "Do you think you'll stay out here awhile? Because Marc and I would like to..."

"Say no more. Yeah, I'll stay here for an hour or two. Shoot me a text when the coast is clear."

"Or you could stay with Caden..."

Quinn rolled her eyes and shook her head. Liz gave her a quick hug before she and Marc left.

The porch emptied, leaving just Caden and Quinn. He looked at her. "Heading back to your room?"

"Not right away. Marc and Liz..."

He grinned. "Right. Do you want company? We could sit in the chairs on the lawn and look at the stars."

"I'd like that." After they sat down, she asked tentatively, "Seeing me dancing with Ian and Marc didn't bother you?"

"No." His voice was firm. "I sat there, waiting for the heart pounding and ear ringing to start, but it didn't. I know neither of them are going after you, but I knew Danny wasn't on New Year's Eve, either, and it didn't make a difference then."

Her heart leaped. "So that's good, right?"

"I think so. It was nice not to have that physical reaction. It's uncomfortable."

They sat quietly for a few minutes, looking at the stars, before Caden spoke again.

"I'm going to tell you something you'll probably find goofy or nerdy. These stars fascinate me, so I downloaded an astronomy app. I wanted to identify the constellations."

"That sounds like fun. Can you point some out to me?"

He laughed. "Sure, but you can be honest. It really is nerdy." He pointed out a couple of constellations and told her how to find them and how the sky would look different when they were back in New England.

"You'll be able to use it on the rooftop terrace."

"Except the stars aren't as bright in Boston."

"Have you had any of those dinner parties?"

"Just one. Right before I left, I invited the gang so I could tell them." He blew out his breath. "It was my first time up there since New Year's weekend."

Quinn considered that, remembering the feel of his arm holding her close to him as they studied the city skyline.

After a few minutes of quiet, Caden asked her what she was thinking about.

"All the times we barely made it in the door to my place or yours before we were tearing each other's clothes off."

He nodded. "I think about those times a lot."

Just then, her cell phone dinged with a text from Liz. "Well, the coast is clear, so I can go to bed. You'll do the beach trip tomorrow? We never made it to the beach."

"Yup, I'll do the beach." They started walking toward the house. "Did you visit your parents in Florida?"

Quinn took several steps before she answered. "Yeah. I didn't want to, but they pushed me, thought I needed a change of scenery. It was awful. I'll see you tomorrow."

Chapter Twenty

Sharing A Lounge Chair

Honduras—The Third Week

Caden

THE BEACH WAS BEAUTIFUL, with white sand and turquoise water. A volleyball court quickly filled with doctors and nurses competing against each other. Caden chose volleyball, while Quinn sunbathed near the water with Liz and Marc.

He glanced over at them, realizing it was his first time seeing Quinn in a bikini. That first morning when she had sent him a bathing suit picture flooded his mind. *Everything was simple then.*

The game ended, and all the players made their way over to the water where Quinn was playing in the waves with Liz. Caden walked into the water, and as he reached them, a wave came up from behind, knocking Quinn off her feet. Caden put his arms out and caught her. She scrambled to regain her footing as another wave swept in, knocking them both over. They came up sputtering and laughing.

Back on the beach, Caden grabbed the sunscreen, slathering it everywhere and looking at Quinn. "Will you do my back?" *I'm playing with fire, but damn, I want to feel her touch.*

She squeezed the sunscreen onto his back and rubbed it in. Instantly he thought back to their times in bed when her hands were all over his body, and he hardened with the memories.

She finished and lay face down on the towel next to him. Her bikini was jade green, and it did nothing to lessen his erection.

Despite the sunscreen, they were all sunburned on the ride back to the clinic.

Tuesday night was Caden's call to his therapist, and she opened the call by saying, "During our session last week, you were going to seek out Quinn. How did that go?"

He relayed the conversations he had with Quinn at the swimming pool and on the drive back from the remote clinic. He told her about the music at the clinic and the dancing. "A doctor came over and pulled her up to dance. I waited for the physical reactions, but they didn't happen. So do your job, doc. Analyze that. Am I cured?"

"Do you think you are?"

"Ohh, answering my question with a question. So frustrating." He liked the rapport he had with her, but the work was hard. She didn't give him anything easily. "Probably not. There was a beach trip on Sunday, and while I was playing volleyball, Quinn was near the water with Liz and Marc. That's Quinn's roommate and her fling. I watched Marc putting sunscreen on them and seeing that started my heart racing. But I didn't spiral."

"Do you think that's because you and Quinn are not together?"

"I've considered that, but every fiber of me wants to be with her, so I don't think so."

"Did you tell her that?"

He replayed their conversations in his mind. "Not in so many words, but I let her know how much I miss her."

"And how did she react?"

"She's afraid." And Caden completely understood that.

"Of you?"

"Not physically. She told me she trusted I would keep her safe on the trip to the remote clinic. She's afraid of starting up only to have me walk away again."

"Do you share her concern?"

Caden snorted. "Of course. I don't want to hurt her again. Or myself."

"You've started being more social than you were the first month. How does that feel?"

"It's good, but it's all tied to Quinn. I don't know if I would do group things if she wasn't here."

They continued to talk, and at the end of their call, she said, "Caden, this was good tonight."

He smiled. "Yeah, it was."

Quinn

Caden worked with other nurses at the start of the week, and while he joined the group for dinner, he hadn't stayed around in the evenings. The trip to the remote clinic and spending time with him over the weekend had fanned Quinn's desire from a spark into a flame, and now she missed him more than ever.

The nights were the worst. Sleep eluded her as she tossed and turned, thinking about being with him. She wanted him physically, but also wanted much more. She longed to hear him call her his girlfriend again, wanted to tell him how much she loved him and make plans for a future together. Her mind drifted back to the second weekend they spent together and how she had wondered by the end if his feelings were as intense as hers. Her emotions felt the same now. She was ready to go all in. Again.

Quinn made her way to the pool on Wednesday night, enjoying the feel of the water against her still slightly sun-burned skin. Concentrating on her breathing and form, she hoped to wipe Caden out of her mind for at least a little while, but as she was drying off, she felt his eyes boring into her back. Turning around, she met his gaze.

"Hi. I've been kind of out of touch since the beach and want to apologize. I've been trying to work through some stuff." Caden was stretched out on one of the old-fashioned loungers. He was wearing shorts, and a faded T-shirt. The sight of his long legs affected Quinn, and she took a deep breath, trying to calm down.

She moved a chair closer, and sat on it, facing him. "Do you want to talk about it?"

"Yeah. Yeah, I do, but I'm not sure it'll make sense. I was a mess after I left you in February. I wasn't sleeping well, had no appetite, and was very short-tempered with everyone. My ther-apist diagnosed anxiety and started me on meds." He paused. "I hated that I couldn't get on top of it on my own. Especially considering it was my decision to walk away. I thought the anxiety started with that first panic attack in December. But I've realized it probably started as soon as I met you."

Quinn cocked her head. "That makes me feel kind of bad. I'd like to think meeting me made you happy."

"Oh my God, it did. But I've known from the minute I met you, this,"—he waved his hand between them — "you and I, was going to be something serious. It would be the first time since Mary that I let myself care. And caring meant worrying about whether you were going to care for me in the same way. Would you cheat? Were you going to be with me because I have money? It all caused anxiety. I just didn't realize until now that it started when we met."

"Is anxiety something separate from panic attacks? You never mentioned anxiety. I always thought you had yourself together—I mean until you didn't. Do the meds help?"

"Somewhat. They let me sleep, at least. The panic attacks are an acute, momentary thing, while the anxiety is always there, hovering in the background. I'm always waiting for a shoe to drop, for something to go wrong."

"Since the very beginning?"

"Yeah."

She took a minute to digest this. "I think that's normal, especially meeting someone of our age. When you're young, you have the immature love you think will last forever, and when it doesn't, that hurts, but you learn you can survive it. When you're older, you're keenly aware of all the pitfalls to putting your heart out there, but you know you'll be okay even if it ends. You know the old saying, 'It's better to have loved and lost than never to have loved at all.'"

He nodded. "I think I'm a little delayed in that department because I was with Mary for so long, and she's the only one I'd ever cared about that deeply. Before you. I know you've had a few times you considered yourself in love."

"Yeah, I learned I could survive being hurt."

"Maybe that's the piece I'm missing. I survived the debacle with Mary, but it was so fucking hard. I never wanted to go through that again, and then I did it to myself by walking away from you." He ran his hand through his hair, a gesture she found so endearing and had missed so much.

"Here's the interesting part." He locked eyes with her. "I nearly jumped out of my skin when Paul introduced you that first day, and I continued to be on edge until I finally talked to you. Now, every time I talk to you, I feel a little calmer." He grinned. "You're a natural antianxiety med for me."

She frowned at him. "I'm that boring, huh?"

"Not at all. I think all the work I've done since February is coming together." He spread his legs and patted the lounger. "Come sit here." When she looked at him warily, he spread his hands. "I only want to be close to you, I promise. Nothing more."

Quinn rose slowly, took a step, then eased herself down between his legs. His arms reached to draw her against him.

Their closeness aroused him—she could feel his growing erection—but he did nothing except keep his arms around her. She sighed and relaxed into him. They sat silently like that for several minutes.

After a moment, she recalled an idea she'd had months earlier. "Have you ever thought about giving away the money? Like to a charity? It's such a big issue for you."

"I give to charity mostly to decrease my taxes." Then she felt him shake his head. "No, that's not right. I have things I give to with no tax benefit, but I also have a financial advisor, and he tells me how much to give to get the maximum benefit. But I sense you're talking bigger than that."

"I'm talking about all of it. You said you don't have student loans. Is the brownstone paid for? And your car? Take care of those and then give away the rest of it. You must make enough money to live comfortably."

"Oh, absolutely." He went silent for a moment. "It's an intriguing idea. My parents instilled the value of work in all of us. That's why none of us are living a jet-set life."

"It's just an idea. Maybe you'd be happier if it was gone." She sighed. "I've missed this." She felt him nod in agreement.

Chapter Twenty-One

When Stars Align

Caden

CADEN WAS WAITING WHEN Quinn climbed out of the pool the next night. As she toweled off, he patted the lounger as he had the night before.

"I'm wet. I'll get you all wet."

He raised his eyebrows at her. "I'm not sugar. I won't melt."

When Quinn sat, he drew her in again. Hearing her mention of being wet, even knowing she meant from swimming, made him think about all the times they'd been together and how wet she would get for him. He grew hard and knew she could feel it against her back. Still, she relaxed against him, which let him know she was okay with it.

Should I tell her about my therapy session?

He swallowed. "I told my therapist your theory about how everyone has anxiety starting relationships."

"And?"

"She asked me what I thought, because that's how she does therapy, answering a question with a question." He took a deep breath before continuing. "I know you're right, but I'm not as far along in that journey. I've been stripping myself bare in therapy since February, and I'm going to be needy, wanting reassurance and handholding until I learn to trust. Maybe I'll lose my way occasionally, but I won't lose myself."

He wanted her to read between the lines. She stiffened when he started talking, but he felt her relax again as he finished.

She reached back and took his hand in hers, and they sat quietly for a few minutes. "If you realize you won't lose yourself, does that mean you understand you are not an abuser?"

He squeezed her hand tightly. "Yes."

Later, Caden lay in bed, thinking about the feel of Quinn against him. When she took his hand, he knew she understood what he was telling her. He didn't know if the PTRS would rear its head again or how he'd handle it.

But I have figured out who I am, and a brief panic attack will not change that.

Quinn

Quinn tossed and turned all night, thinking about what Caden had said at the pool. *If he recognizes he's not an abuser, does it mean we could reunite? Does he want reassurance and handholding from me?*

She had that same feeling of a bubble growing inside that she had described to him on Christmas Eve. Her love for him was overwhelming, but she didn't know if it was enough.

Saturday was Marc's last night in Honduras before leaving early Sunday morning to return to New Jersey. Quinn knew Liz was going to miss him, and she wondered if they'd try to keep the relationship going. South Carolina to New Jersey was a lot farther than Boston to Hanover.

As the four of them shared one last dinner together, Caden asked Marc if he would ever come to Honduras again.

"I'd like to. It's been a great experience, life-changing, but I don't see the stars aligning for me to do it again. Certainly not for such an extended period."

"Stars aligning?"

"All the pieces came together to give me the two-month window to come down here." Marc smiled. "I applied for and was hired for a new job, which starts on August fifteenth. That was in May, and I thought I'd stay in my old job until, well, right around now. A week later, the hospital downsized, and my position was cut. I knew it might happen, which was why I applied for the other job. Then my girlfriend broke up with me, and I had to leave our apartment. I had a mini midlife crisis. At twenty-nine."

He laughed. "This program kept invading my thoughts, and I finally decided it was time to try it. I'll probably never have a two-month window with no job or financial obligations again. The stars aligned."

Liz said she felt the same way about her journey to Honduras. They'd discovered mold in her wing of the hospital in Charleston, and the remediation would take three months, so they gave the staff for that wing a paid leave while it was taking place.

"Three months paid?" Quinn asked. "Wow."

"I know, it's crazy." Liz shrugged. "The hospital didn't want to lose the staff. If the remediation takes longer, we'll be able to go on unemployment and the hospital will continue our health insurance. Like Marc, I'd looked at this program. I figured I'd never get another chance to do it. The stars aligned for me too. It's unlikely I'll ever be able to afford to do it again. How about you, Quinn?"

"I never thought of my trip here as the stars aligning," she admitted. "I'd finished my master's program and was at loose ends. The hospital encourages humanitarian work, and I had enough money to pay my bills for a month, so I applied. I don't know if I'll ever be able to take a life pause like this again." She looked around at them. "But I totally agree with Marc—it's been life-changing. It's easy to get stuck in the rut of everyday life. Everyone ought to do something like this."

Liz nodded. "Your turn, doc. Did the stars align to bring you here?"

Caden glanced at Quinn before answering. "I didn't think of it in those terms. I thought I might benefit from a change in location since I've lived my entire life in Boston. This is the longest I've been away from the city. I've seen a whole different world. The quiet and the stars are incredible. The two months here have done everything I hoped for and more. I'd agree with life changing."

Liz poured the last of the bottle of wine and raised her glass in a toast. "To life-changing experiences." They clinked their glasses, then Liz looked at Marc. "Let's head up to your room for the last time." She turned to Quinn. "His transport to the airport is early, and I'm going to ride with him. I'll see you sometime tomorrow."

They all stood, and Marc hugged Quinn, saying, "I'm glad I met you."

She hugged him back without thinking. "It's not that far from New Jersey to New England. You can visit." When the hug ended, she looked toward Caden, wondering about his reaction. He seemed fine. She recalled their conversation the night he left her, when she told him she wouldn't do things to trigger him.

He was right. We don't even know what the triggers are, and I can't live continually on edge about it.

Marc shook Caden's hand. "Take it easy, doc. I bet there's somewhere you can see the stars without coming all the way to Honduras."

Caden laughed. "You're right, but it's probably not New Jersey. Good luck with the new job."

Caden asked Quinn if she was going swimming, and she told him she didn't usually on the weekends. "Let's go down there and sit anyway," he suggested. "I have something I want to run by you." Quinn said they could sit by the fire pit, but he shook his head. "We could, but I like those loungers by the pool. I enjoy sitting with you close to me."

When they arrived at the pool, Caden asked, "Will you sit with me again?" Quinn nodded, and he pulled her close as they sat down. He started, "I've..."

Quinn interrupted him. "I need to ask you something first."

"Okay." His tone was wary, and she knew it was because of how forcefully she'd stopped him.

"Me hugging Marc back there. It didn't bother you?"

"No."

She sighed, and Caden shifted so he could see her face. "What's going on?"

"I remembered what you said that night about triggers and I don't want to do that. But I didn't even think about it."

"And you shouldn't have to. Quinn, I won't ask you to live that way. It's not realistic. I'm going to conquer this, or..." His words trailed away.

"Or what?"

"I don't know. There is no other scenario. I'm better and I'm going to continue on that track." He ran his hand through his hair. "This might not be the right time to tell you what I'm thinking about."

She took his hand. "Please do. I'm sorry I interrupted you, but we need to be open, and I felt like you needed to know what I was thinking."

"I want that. Brutal honesty." He smiled at her. "I've been thinking about your suggestion that I give the money away. I have some things I'd want to do first, and then I want to control where it goes."

She looked back at him. "Not sure I understand."

"I want to start a foundation so I know where the money goes. And while I was listening to the three of you talk tonight, it made me realize that because of financial restraints, people who want to do this kind of work can't." He took a breath. "I don't have all the details worked out yet, but I want to help people experience this. It can't be heavy on admin. I want the money to go where it will truly make a difference."

"Do you know anything about setting up a foundation?"

"No, but I think we can figure it out." He paused. "I'd like you to be a part of it. You and Liz both mentioned finances. I know how this sounds, but the idea of not being able to afford to come here wasn't something that I had to think about. I need your perspective."

She was quiet for a few minutes before she answered. "It's an intriguing idea."

"I don't have it all fleshed out, but the idea of putting it together is exciting. I hope you'll work on it with me."

She nodded. "I've never been involved in anything like that. Let me think about it."

The silence enveloped them as the stars twinkled overhead. Eventually, the evening grew chilly, and they stood to leave.

Quinn took Caden's hand. She gazed into his eyes, and they moved toward each other. When he embraced her, she melted against him. After several minutes, she pulled back and stood on tiptoes, gently kissing him.

Neither of them tried to take it any further, but Caden put his hand on her hair and drew her head to his chest. "I've missed this."

She felt his smile. "So have I."

$$Chapter\ Twenty\text{-}Two$$

Reunion

Honduras—The Fourth Week

Quinn

"Nothing since Saturday night?" Mya and Quinn were sitting on the porch after dinner on Tuesday night. The week before, Quinn had shared the story of her past with Caden, and when Mya asked about him at dinner, Quinn had to admit that she hadn't talked to him since Saturday.

"He asked me to work with him on starting a foundation. I kissed him and haven't heard a peep since."

"Was it a 'How exciting to work on something like that' type of kiss or something else?" Mya looked expectantly at Quinn.

"Something else." Quinn blushed, and when Mya raised her eyebrows, she said, "It was an 'I've missed you like crazy for months and I need you to touch me,' kiss."

"You scared him away."

"I didn't think so. It wasn't aggressive, and we both admitted we've missed it." Quinn stretched her arms over her head. "Enough about me. How are you doing?"

Mya had gone back to see the orthopedist that morning. "It's healing well. Another couple of weeks in the sling, then he'll set me free." Most of her bruises had faded away, and the clinic had her working on intake. "I'm going to miss you. I'm sorry we never got to do more hiking."

"Come and visit me before you go back to New Zealand. New England in the fall is beautiful. Maybe you'll decide you want to stay."

The clinic day had wound down on Wednesday afternoon, leaving one last patient whom Caden was examining. Quinn watched him work, thinking about how her time in Honduras was ending. She'd be returning to New Hampshire on Saturday, on the same flight as Caden.

Her intention in coming to Honduras had been to get over him, and she was no closer to that than she had been in February. The foundation he wanted to start sounded fascinating, and his desire for her to be a part of it was flattering, but it would mean regular contact. There had been nothing between them since the chaste kiss on Saturday night, and Quinn wondered if Mya was right and she had scared him away.

I can't see him regularly if we are only friends. She just could not do it.

Caden finished with the patient and started helping Quinn clean up. "I've been trying to keep my distance," he said.

She jerked her head up. "I've noticed." She gave him a minute to respond, and when he didn't, she asked, "Why?"

"I don't want to push you. I..." Before he could finish, a car careened into the parking lot.

The driver jumped out and dashed to the passenger side, crying, "Help me, help me," in Spanish. He yanked a young boy out of the car, cradled him in his arms, and ran toward Caden, still crying for help.

The boy was bleeding profusely from his abdomen. Caden extended his arms to take the boy and laid him on a table. He questioned the man in Spanish, asking what happened and the boy's name.

As the man answered, Caden translated so Quinn would know what was going on. "It's his son. His name is José, and he's been shot." Caden continued to interrogate the man in Spanish and shook his head in frustration. "He won't tell me how it happened."

Quinn drew in a sharp breath, and Caden continued, "It's not important. Let's go. Get me all the lap pads you can find, plus suture and surgical kits."

Quinn ran to the supply closet and gathered everything Caden asked for, as well as an IV setup. Another car raced into the lot, and the man who jumped out of it charged into the clinic. He brandished a weapon as he screamed at the boy's father, who snatched a handgun from the waistband of his pants.

Quinn was almost back to the exam area when the second man grabbed her. He jammed the gun into her back and started yelling words she didn't understand. The boy's father yelled back at him.

Caden started talking calmly but firmly in Spanish. Quinn understood most of it. "I need her here right now. Back away." The man started pushing her toward Caden, still yelling. Caden spoke again a little more loudly, "I need her now. I need those supplies. This boy needs attention if he's going to live. Back away from her so she can help me."

The man let Quinn go, but stayed close behind her. She moved to the table and started rapidly handing Caden lap pads.

She asked if he wanted her to start an IV, and he nodded. Her hands were shaking, and she wasn't sure how the stick would go, but after taking a couple of deep breaths, she was successful on the first try.

The second man was directly behind her with the gun aimed at her back. Caden asked for her help in turning the boy over. "There's no exit wound," he whispered.

"So, is the bullet still inside?"

"Yes. I can't understand everything they're saying. Maybe it's family related?" The doctors and nurses who had been on the porch of the manse gathered as they heard the commotion in the clinic. The second man waved his gun threateningly at the crowd, warning them to stay back.

"Paul, I could use you here," Caden said. As Paul moved in, the gun was stuck in Quinn's back again. "No," Caden said firmly. "I need her. Let her go!"

The man let her go, but Quinn could still feel him close behind her as she moved back to the table to assist. Caden located the bullet and started the repair with help from Paul and Quinn.

The security guard and the driver were approaching, and Quinn silently prayed. *Please, please, please, no gunshots. Please, please, please, let them get these guys, please, please, please.*

As Caden was finishing, she felt the security guard grab the gunman from behind her while the driver took control of the other man. They dragged them to the opposite end of the clinic.

"He needs to go to the hospital," Caden said. "I stitched what I could find, but there could be more damage. What are they going to do with them?" His head jerked toward the two men.

Paul said they would transport them to the city police, and Caden asked if they could take the boy too.

"We have a vehicle that's bigger than the jeep," Paul said. "I think we can fit everyone in it. We'll need a doctor to go."

He looked at Caden, who shook his head.

Paul nodded. "I'll do it."

Quinn stood silently listening to the conversation, quaking inside, still feeling the gun on her back.

Caden looked at her. "We need to talk to security to figure out the logistics of getting him to the hospital. Are you okay monitoring him?"

Not trusting herself to talk, she nodded silently. Quinn could tell he didn't want to leave her, but Paul wanted his help to get the transport organized. She watched as Caden looked around and caught Liz's eye. He motioned toward Quinn.

Liz walked over to Quinn. "Let's get things cleaned up a little." That was exactly what Quinn needed, something to focus on.

She told Liz, "They're trying to figure out transportation to the hospital."

"Are they going to take those two as well?"

"I think so."

"They'll have to hog-tie them. I doubt they have handcuffs. Are they going to take a doctor or a nurse?"

"Paul said he'd go. You don't plan to volunteer for that, do you?"

"Oh, hell no. Watching you guys filled my excitement quotient for a long time."

They worked as they were talking, and it calmed Quinn more than she thought possible.

A few minutes later, a transport van appeared in the parking lot, and Liz was right—the two men had their hands tied behind their backs and their feet bound. They had put a mattress in the back of the van, and Caden was carrying blankets to them.

"Can the two of you wrap the boy in these? Paul and Ian are going in the van. We've called the hospital, and they are going to dispatch an ambulance. They'll handle it the same as we did when Mya was injured, except today, after the boy is transferred to the ambulance, the van will continue to the police station."

The boy moaned softly as Quinn and Liz wrapped him in the blankets. When they finished, Caden and Paul lifted him into the van.

One of the doctors said, "Well done, all of you," and the crowd applauded.

Caden shook his head. "We'll be happy to let someone else have the next one."

The van left, and the crowd headed back to the manse.

Liz looked at Quinn. "Are you okay? Is there anything I can do?"

Quinn told Liz she'd be fine, and Caden nodded. With a final glance, Liz left them alone.

Caden walked over to Quinn and put his arms around her. It released her emotions, and she began shaking, much like the night she'd told him about sleeping with Sam in Boston.

"You're okay," Caden said. "You did an amazing job."

Her eyes filled with tears, and she fought to hold back sobs.

"It's okay, you can cry. I get it." His voice was soft.

She gave up and buried her head against his chest, crying in big, gulping sobs. Caden picked her up and walked to the chairs by the fire pit, where he sat down and settled her in his lap.

The crying didn't last long, but the shaking continued, and Caden held her tightly until it stopped.

Finally, she lifted her head and looked at him. "My God, Caden, I've never been that scared."

"You hid it well. You did exactly what I needed. It scared me too. I was so fucking afraid I was going to lose you."

"Have you been through something like that before?"

"Yeah, a few times in Boston. Security was always on top of it. These guys did a great job." He let out a long sigh and ran his hand through his hair, shaking his head.

Quinn wiped the remaining tears from her face. "I discovered I'm more religious than I thought, because I was praying I wouldn't hear gunshots when security was going after them."

"So was I. 'There are no atheists in foxholes.' I believe it now."

"Me too. This is going to take a bit of time to get over."

"For me too." Caden cupped her cheeks in his hands and stared into her eyes. "Quinn, I love you, and I want us back. Today, I truly thought I would never get the chance to tell you that. I'm sorry for the pain I caused you. Can you forgive me? I want to spend the rest of my life with you."

Those were the words she'd been wanting to hear. She paused before answering, thinking about how she still tried to heed her mother's long-ago words about not making decisions in the heat of emotion.

But sometimes you must throw caution to the wind. She'd made her decision already.

She smiled. "Caden, I never stopped loving you. I tried, but I couldn't. I only need to know that no matter what happens, we'll work through it together."

"Yes." He smiled. "Yes. Stay with me for our last few nights here. I don't want to let you out of my sight. And when we get back to Boston, we'll figure out the rest of it."

He kissed her, and just like their first, she felt it in her toes. Standing, he wrapped his arms around her, and Quinn relished the feel of him against her, drinking in the heat rising from both of them.

After a moment, he murmured, "I don't even care that we don't have a condom. I want—no, I need to be with you. And I mean *now*. If we end up with a baby, it's perfectly fine. More than fine."

His words amped up her desire, and she kissed him passionately before pulling back and giving him a coy smile. "There are condoms here. Trust your nurse to know where the supplies are."

The End

Epilogue

Quinn

QUINN PULLED HER ROLLER bag through the airport doors and turned back for one last wave to the driver from the clinic. Her eyes grew misty, although nothing compared to the tears she had shed saying goodbye to everyone before embarking on the long drive. Mya had been the most difficult, although she was already making plans to visit Quinn in September. And Quinn knew saying goodbye to Liz, who was trailing along beside her, would be even worse. She turned her attention inside, looking for her airline.

Caden came from behind as she was tagging her bag. He bent and kissed the back of her neck. "I'm going to the desk to see if they will change our seats, so we're together. Can I leave my bag here with you?"

"Of course. Do you want me to tag it?"

"Nope, I'll be right back." He kissed her again.

Quinn smiled, watching him walk away. They'd had three amazing nights since the incident on Wednesday. And the days hadn't been bad either, as Quinn found herself in a constant state of arousal. One glance between them at the clinic quickly ramped up to a smoldering fire between her legs. This wasn't at all the conclusion she'd expected when she boarded the plane in Boston four weeks ago, but she couldn't deny it was the one she longed for.

"Oh my God, more of the googly eyes between you." Liz printed her tag. "It's enough to make someone ill. I can't wait to get on my plane to Atlanta." Her teasing had been non-stop since the night Quinn went to Caden's room. "I still say you should have gotten together the first week you were here, so Marc and I could have had the room for the entire month. But no. you had to wait until after he left." She wrapped the tag around the handle of her suitcase, then looked up with tears in her eyes. Throwing her arms around Quinn, she said, "I'm going to miss you so much."

Quinn blinked back her own tears as Liz held her. "Same girl, same. My door's always open and I know Cade's is, too. Come and visit anytime."

Liz took a deep breath, trying to compose herself. "The planes fly both ways. You better be coming to Charleston, too."

"I will, I promise."

Caden returned and wrapped his arms around Liz. "You have a safe trip. And don't be a stranger."

"I won't." Her plane was boarding and as Liz was verifying her boarding group, her name was called over the loudspeaker. "What in the world?" She looked at Quinn and Caden, confusion showing on her face.

Caden said, "You better go see what they want. It's never good to ignore those kinds of calls." As she walked toward the gate, he slung his arm over Quinn's shoulder. "Shall we go to our gate?"

Quinn nodded as she watched Liz step into the swirl of travelers waiting to board. She turned with a wide smile and although Quinn couldn't hear her over the din, she could read her lips. "Did you see that, Cade? She got upgraded to First Class!"

Without saying a word, Caden hugged her closer to him as they walked through the airport. Their flight was boarding, and he said, "I think this is us." He handed Quinn her boarding pass.

"Oh my God. You did this, didn't you? We're in first class too." Quinn grasped his arm. "Did you upgrade Liz?"

He nodded with a satisfied smile. "Might as well use that money for something fun," he confided as they bumped along the jetport.

A flight attendant greeted them. "Good afternoon, Dr. Brady, Ms. Michaels. We'll bring drinks as soon as you are settled. What would you like?"

Quinn looked at Caden, her eyes wide, and he grinned at her as he answered. "Two shots of Jameson. Is that okay with you, babe?"

When they reached the third row, Caden lifted first his roller bag and then Quinn's into the overhead compartment. She slid into the window seat and moaned with pleasure. "Do you know how many flights I've taken where I was squished between two people, unable to move? This is heavenly."

Caden settled beside her and immediately raised the armrest between them. Their drinks arrived, and he tapped his against Quinn's. "To a much more pleasant flight than the one down here was."

"Amen to that. I slept a good share of it. It was so hard being in Boston."

Caden leaned over to kiss her. "I know. I haven't seen Claire since you and I saw them in February. Rory's eight months old. But I couldn't go up there, knowing you would be so close." He stroked her cheek, making her look at him. "Never again." They explored every inch of their seats, trying out every gadget.

Caden whispered in her ear. "I wish these seats would lie flat. We could join the mile high club."

"Maybe when we take that trip to Ireland and France." Quinn cocked her head. "Although, if you put all the money into a foundation, will we be able to do this?"

"You're entirely too practical." The attendant brought blankets, offered them another drink and said lunch would be served soon.

They dined on curried butternut squash soup, olive and feta stuffed chicken breast with potato au gratin, and passion fruit mousse cake for dessert. Caden sighed. "This is fantastic. Maybe I'll keep a contingency fund for first class flights." With dinner finished, they reclined their seats and when Quinn leaned against his shoulder, Caden pulled the blanket up to their chins and buried his head in her hair. "A new doctor started a few weeks before I left Boston. She wore the same scent that you do. It killed me every time she walked by." He was rubbing her back as he talked, and his hand wandered to the hem of her shirt, then slowly made its way to her breasts.

"We can't have sex here," she whispered. "Can we?"

"I'll behave if you do." He sought her lips and kissed her until she let a yawn escape.

"I'm sorry." Quinn laughed. "That wine with lunch made me sleepy." She snuggled against his shoulder. "It was hard to leave, but now that we're on our way, I can't wait to be home."

"We haven't talked much about what's going to happen at home."

"I know." She looked chagrined. "Between work, goodbyes and making love, we kind of back-burnered that. I have a week before I go back to work, and since we already decided I'll spend that in Boston, we'll have time to figure it out." She yawned again and her eyes were heavy.

"Move in with me," Caden murmured.

"I can't." Quinn answered as she was dozing off.

Caden

He'd been wanting to ask her to move in since they climbed the stairs to his room three nights ago, but she was right. Everything else had come before discussions of their future. Contentment washed over him as he held her, listening to her even breathing. He knew what he wanted the future to look like, married to Quinn, living in Boston and kids. He also knew it was way too soon to be having those thoughts. *Damn it. Why did I ask her to move in?* He gazed at her face, remembering all the emotions he'd seen. The anticipation on their first date, the blush on her cheeks the first time he massaged her feet, her delight when they visited the Christmas Village, the throes of passion when they made love, compassion when he told her about his grandfather's death, devastation when he left her in February, the shock when she saw him in Honduras and her steely calm that afternoon in the clinic. *Maybe she won't remember.*

Quinn's eyes fluttered open as Caden was scrolling on his phone. "That's the best sleep I ever had on a plane. What are you looking at?"

"Nothing special." He swiped the phone to the home screen. *Dare I suggest it?*

"Cade." She placed her palm on his cheek. "I'm not ready to walk away from my life in New Hampshire."

Shit. "I understand."

"I'm glad you do, because I'm not sure I do." She chuckled. "I love you and I want to be with you. But I love my life in New Hampshire, my friends, my job, my townhouse. I'm not ready to give all of that up." She closed her eyes and when she opened them, she looked straight into Caden's. "What if this doesn't work out? It's been three days..."

"You're afraid I'll flip out again."

"Not really. We've talked that out. But I've never lived with anyone. And yes, I'm scared."

"Quinn, I want more than we had before. Dinner once a week and every other weekend, if we can work that out, won't be enough."

"I want more too."

Caden took a deep breath. "What if we tweak our schedules? Swap out some day shifts for evenings? Work three twelves? And one of us travels to the other. We'll have sleepovers." He grinned. "Obviously, I don't have all the details of what it could look like, but that's what I was thinking about while you napped. I know you don't want to give up the monthly dinners with your tribe, or swimming with Izzy."

"And you shouldn't give up Friday nights at O'Malley's. I want our relationship to add to our lives, not subtract."

Caden nodded. "We can spend the week working on this. It's easy for me. I have a lot of input to the schedule, but what about you?"

"I shouldn't have any problem switching to evenings for some shifts." She shifted closer to him. "We're *going* to make this work."

"We are. Here's one more idea and if you don't like it, tell me. My hospital has a program where we swap out personnel with another hospital, usually a smaller one in a rural area. We send people to the rural hospital for two months and they send people to us." He looked at her expectantly. "An exchange with Hanover is going to start this fall. You could come to Boston for October and November, stay with me, try it out." He liked the smile blossoming across her face. "And then in the winter, I'd come to Hanover and stay with you."

"You'd leave Boston? I mean, you aren't thinking about leaving the hospital permanently, are you?"

"Maybe." He cocked his head. "Honduras was a drastic, monumental change for me, and it was good. Even before you arrived." He kissed her. "The conditions were challenging with limited resources, but it was fulfilling and much less stressful than I'm used to. I'd like to see what it's like in a fully equipped, first-class hospital but out of the pressure cooker of the city."

"You'd actually consider moving to Hanover?" Disbelief was etched all over her face.

"I would. If we decide that's the best place for us." Caden studied her face. "Do you like the idea?"

"I love it! Spending two months in Boston with you, without having to sever my ties to Hanover, is huge. And I love the idea of you spending two months with me. There's so much you haven't seen yet." Quinn looked out the window. "There's the skyline. We're almost home."

"Yes, we are." Caden clasped her hands and leaned over to watch the city come into focus. "I love you."

Afterword

Did you enjoy this book? If you did, leaving a review on Amazon or Goodreads is a wonderful way to let the author know. Reviews are one of the most powerful tools in an author's arsenal.

Sneak Peak

Sam Carpenter turned onto the winding dirt road, his good mood from that afternoon ebbing away. Not even the surprise reunion with Quinn Michaels, his first love, was enough to ward off the despondence that had been nipping at him since he left Boston. The drive home had been long, and as Sam pulled up to his very dark house, despair engulfed him.

It was not supposed to be like this. His daughter Piper should be opening the door and jumping into his arms, shouting about how much she missed him. In his fantasy world, all trace of her stutter would be gone. When he'd planned the trip, Sam hoped that the time apart would ease the differences between him and Piper's mother, Norah, his partner of eight years. That theory didn't even get to be tested. Instead, five days earlier, as he walked out the door, Norah had told him she and Piper wouldn't be there when he returned.

Sam climbed out of the car slowly, digging the key from his pocket. He hesitated to open the door—walking into that empty house would make it all real. Norah had called the day before and told him she had moved out everything that she'd brought into their home, including Piper's bed. Finally, his shaking hand worked the lock, and the door swung open. On autopilot, he flipped a switch, and light flooded the mudroom. " At least she didn't take the light bulbs," he muttered, dropping his duffle and backpack to the floor.

Wandering into the kitchen, Sam noticed a colorful stone he'd found on the first hike he and Norah had taken over eight years ago, sitting on the counter. "What the...She kept that on her desk."

When he walked closer, he saw the rock was anchoring a note.

S

The house I've rented is at 106 Rock Maple Road

I hate that we've come to this, but the tension between us has become intolerable. I can't watch our precious little girl sink any lower because of our actions. I know, in the depths of your heart, you feel the same way.

My lease is for six months. Maybe that will be long enough...

I'll always love you.

N

Sam propped his elbow on the counter and lowered his forehead to his fist, still gripping the note in his other hand. After a few moments, he straightened, crumpled the paper into a ball, and opened the cabinet where they kept a wastebasket, only to find it empty. He shook his head. "Of course. Everything is gone." He tossed the scrunched-up note into a corner of the kitchen.

Sam made his way through the house, opening the kitchen cabinets to find only a few plates and bowls, a couple of pots and pans, a coffee mug and two glasses. The dining room was empty, but the living room still had the couch, recliner and television—all things Sam had purchased. Both his bedroom and Piper's were completely devoid of furniture.

A trip back to the car yielded bedding purchased on his way home, as well as a six-pack of beer, a takeout pizza, and a sack of groceries. The bedding joined his backpack on the floor. Sam took the pizza and a can of beer into the living room and sank down onto the couch, where he popped the top of the beer and took a long swallow.

Looking around, Sam rubbed his hand over his jaw. *Damn.* He shook his head. *I'm thirty-one years old and have nothing to show for it.* He took another sip of his beer. *Except for Piper.* He would always have her.

His bite of pizza caught in his throat, and he shoved the rest of the slice back into the box. He chugged the beer, and in a sudden fit of despair, he threw the can across the room. As it bounced off the opposite wall, echoing in the hollowness of the room, Sam rested his elbows on his knees and dropped his head into his hands, emotionally exhausted...

After a few minutes, Sam rose and walked to the kitchen with a heavy tread. He stood at the island, staring at the ball of paper in the corner, mocking him. Taking a deep breath, he picked it up and smoothed it out on the counter. *106 Rock Maple. She isn't far from here.* He drank another beer standing at the counter, trying to figure a path forward.

Another can called his name, and he reached for it, then pulled back. *Pip's going to be here in the morning. I need to be ready.*

Sam's fingers ran over the words on the paper as if trying to feel them. He picked up the rock that Norah had placed on top of the note. He could picture her picking up the pen and starting to write, then pausing, raising the pen to her face and tapping it on her chin as she thought about the words she would use. He'd seen her do that hundreds of times.

Then, before she walked out the door for the final time, she took the stone, *their* stone, and placed it on top of the paper.

Damn it, Norah! How do you do this to me? I thought I had clarity, and now I'm tied up in knots—again. He picked up the note and shoved it in a drawer.

Find out what the future holds for Sam in Whispers of Healing, coming on March 13, 2025

Also by Sue Mills

Whispers of Goodbye

Whispers of Forgiveness

Whispers of Mistletoe

Acknowledgements

I hope you enjoyed Quinn and Caden's story. You'll see them again in future books, although not in starring roles.

There are many people who contributed to Whispers of Starlight. First, thank you to my early readers, Melinda Domings, Rebecca Maeve Hartwell of Hart Bound Editing and Deborah Ann Neary.

Also thanks to my daughter Katie. Whenever I wondered how a twenty-nine year old woman might act, she was my go-to source. She also shared her Spotify account with me and made suggestions for Quinn and Caden's playlist. I'm grateful to my brother Jason Meilleur who spent many years as a paramedic and answers all my medical questions.

My critique partners, Sally Walker and Sheryl Soffer gave me valuable insights. I learned so much from our association.

Thanks to my content editor, Rashida Breen and my line editor, Mary Morris, both from Red Adept Editing. Their efforts made my words sing.

I can't say enough about Emily Hensley of Small Fry Marketing. I love what we're creating.

My husband Gordy becomes more involved and more supportive every day and I love having him by my side.

And finally, to my readers. I appreciate you spending some of your reading time with my books and hope you enjoy the stories as much as I do.

About the author

SUE IS AN AVID reader who ventured into the writing world during the first year of the Pandemic. Her stories showcase men and women working to become whole and happy. Family plays a prominent role as do the steamy encounters which come with falling in love.

Sue is a lifelong Vermonter who counts books, sunsets, and travel as vital to her being. Mountains, from the slopes of Vermont's Green Mountains to the towering peaks of Colorado's Rockies feed her soul.

Her children are grown and flown and she's living her happily ever after with the boy she met in a college library fifty years ago.

Follow her on Facebook, Sue Mills – Author https://www.facebook.com/suemillsauthor

Or on her website, suemillsauthor.com https://www.suem
illsauthor.com/books/

Or on Instagram, suemillsauthor

And TikTok, Sue Mills, Author https://www.tiktok.com/
@suemillsauthor